MINDSCAPE ONE

QUEEN'S GAMBIT
KNIGHT & PAWN

OUTLANDERS OF THE MULTIVERSE
COLLECTION

BY D.N. LEO

Narrative Land Publishing
Narrativeland.com

PART ONE

QUEEN'S GAMBIT

CHAPTER 1

Did the gray, dull, and inanimate garden wall in front of her just shiver, sweat, and leak out tears of blood?

This was incredulous. She wasn't Alice in Wonderland. Madeline shook her head. It must be fatigue. She looked at the wall again.

Now, it stood still as any dull gray wall in any backyard. She sighed. It was fatigue.

A strange shade of gray light spread over a garden of plastic-looking trees. Her eyes shot to the sky and widened. She was looking at the magnificent sunset in Eudaiz, a universe far away from Earth.

She smiled.

After what felt like decades of bloodbath and battles, she had survived and come here. The sunset was comforting.

Madeline had read many science fiction novels, which at the moment served the sole purpose of preventing her from freaking out or making a complete idiot of herself.

Then she realized the sunset in front of her was artificial.

The smile left her face, giving way to a frown of anxiety at the daunting thought of an uncertain future.

A few months ago, she would have laughed at the idea that she would ever space travel. But this was worse. She hadn't just space-traveled to get here. She had traveled across dimensions of time and space and God-knows-whatever-else. The sort of travel that didn't allow her to use a map to track the routes, the kind where she didn't know where she had been or how long it had taken her.

In 2015, she had been an accomplished New York journalist. A few short months later, she'd discovered she was not Madeline Roux, but Madeline Kelley. She was only half human from her mother's side because her father was Eudaizian.

She'd met Ciaran in London and discovered that she could love a man like madness. Ciaran said they were soulmates. But his words were too polished for her. She preferred to say simply that they loved each other. She'd married him a few days ago—in whatever dimension existed between Earth and this place.

She was now Madeline LeBlanc, in whatever year it was in Eudaiz.

Eudaiz was a multi-billion citizen universe, governed by a council of nine Sciphils—a word that stood for Scientist Philosopher. There had been countless times Madeline rolled her eyes internally when she used the term.

In her lay English, she considered the council to be like royalty or a government of some kind. They controlled everything in Eudaiz. What intrigued her most was that the council members were mostly humans who'd come from Earth. A council of nine humans governing an immense universe of alien citizens was a concept she'd never have imagined in her wildest dreams.

The thing was, her grandfather had been Sciphil One. Before he died, he'd appointed her as his successor of the Sciphil One position because she was the last living member of her family. So she was due to take up that appointment in a few days and became Sciphil One. That had been quite a shock to her peaceful life on Earth.

Suddenly her vision wavered. The garden in front of her flickered. "Oh, no," she muttered and turned around to go inside. On Earth, she'd thought she was a pseudo psychic. But since reconnecting with her biological family and accepting this Sciphil One position, her psychic ability had become stronger.

She could see minds and track minds, and sometimes she could even read people's minds. The baggage that came along with that ability was that she had precognition—mostly in regards to negative incidents. They called that her talent. She called it a curse.

She didn't think she could make it back inside the house. It seemed as if the ground was moving under her feet.

On the wall at the other side of the garden, a blood-red text appeared: *ENNEAD WILL KILL YOU ALL.*

The garden bed was covered in blood and gore. Body parts littered the ground.

She wanted to run, but her feet were buried in what looked like bricks made of dried bones. She yanked at her feet but couldn't free them. She called out for Ciaran, but no sound escaped her mouth. The bones built themselves up quickly, now reaching up to her body.

She was suffocating in a tomb of bone.

CHAPTER 2

"**W**elcome home," Kyle Wolf muttered to himself.

Kyle drew in the purified air of Eudaiz to remind himself of what he had missed in his thirty-three years living in exile. He swore to his soul that he would make those responsible for his miseries pay. In this universe—or in the one that contained Earth—his soul was the only possession he was sure was not illusory.

He chuckled at his analogy. As a mind-bender, Kyle's strongest talent was the ability to make others hallucinate. He could control people's minds. And he enjoyed doing it, especially when he made people kill themselves.

The stench of fresh blood always gave him a shiver of pleasure.

Deep in his thought, he tripped on a tub of water. He stared at his reflection in the purified water someone had put out in front of their house to give blessings for the new king of Eudaiz. The face mirrored back at him was a face he hadn't dared to look at for a long time—scarred, wrinkled, and ancient.

He had once possessed the typical angelic, Eudaizian look—and he'd had an innocent Eudaizian mind to match.

Those precious days were long gone.

Eudaiz was a place of happiness where people lived in total contentment and excelled at their individual talents. Eudaizians looked like extraordinarily beautiful humans. People here were born beautiful and saw nothing but beauty in their lives. There was no concept of heaven or hell because those benchmarks just weren't needed. This universe offered its citizens a true happiness that no other universe could.

Kyle cursed to himself and glanced from a distance at the happy crowds preparing for the king's coronation. Only those like him who had visited other universes could understand and appreciate Eudaiz, just as only those who had been to hell would appreciate heaven.

Kyle knew the difference between heaven and hell all too well. Eudaiz was a heaven—a perfect world that had rejected him.

"That should be *my* coronation," Kyle mumbled.

Eudaiz's constitution stated that people deserved happiness when they used their excellence to contribute to virtuous acts. But no one had ever clearly defined what a virtuous act was, and more importantly, what it was not.

Kyle clenched his teeth, thinking of the LeBlancs again. His life's work was down the drain now.

Bran LeBlanc, the previous king of Eudaiz, had cut off his eudqi—the life force that gave him his good looks and invincible strength. And Ciaran LeBlanc. Even the sound of the name made him feel as if his head was going to explode. Ciaran had taken the king's sovereignty. And that would terminate Kyle's existence.

"No!" He couldn't let that happen. "Damn you all. I curse you all," he growled. He whirled around in anger. "Ennead will kill you all. I swear to the gods of darkness, I will make them pay. The ennead will kill them all . . ."

A Eudaizian man carrying a tub of purifying water stepped out from a house and ran straight into Kyle. Half of the water in the tub poured out onto Kyle. Putting the tub down, the man turned to check on him.

He caught Kyle's face and withdrew slightly. Then he spoke politely in Eudaizian, "I apologize."

Kyle smiled. He understood that no one in Eudaiz was as ugly as he now was. Of course, the man was shocked seeing his deformed face. Kyle answered in his native tongue. "It's not a problem. I'm on my way to the Sciphil zone. I shouldn't arrive like this." He pointed at a few leaves and flower petals still hanging from his clothes. "May I use your facility to wash up?"

"Oh, of course. You're from the Sciphil council. My house is your house." The man pushed the door open and invited Kyle in.

Kyle shook his head. Naive Eudaizians should die. Kyle followed the man in and closed the door behind him.

Sensing something unusual, the man turned around and looked at Kyle. Kyle savored the fear in the man's eyes and the pain in his voice when he ripped the man's heart out with his bare hand. Kyle wiped the blood from his hand on the man's clothes.

He moved to the window and peeked outside. The air was filled with the distant sounds of cheering, music, and laughter. The aroma of burnt incense and fresh flowers whirled in the air for a moment and was then whisked away by the wind.

"Long live the king!" he hummed the words in his throat and smirked.

CHAPTER 3

Ciaran searched the garden and found Madeline fainted on the ground. His wife scared the hell out of him sometimes. He could see nothing unusual in the garden. The plantation in the garden looked plastic, but having dealt with chemicals for such a long time, he recognized that the material was organic, just not of Earth.

He knew for sure that the dome above that looked like sky was artificial. Its purpose was to create an environment that a human body could tolerate. The air inside the dome was normal. There were no strange creatures here or anything in the garden that he could peg as a sign of danger. *So why had Madeline fainted?*

He looked back at the house. It was more like a grand mansion than a bunker or a stereotypical space residence. Ciaran smiled to himself. Bran was Irish. It was only natural he'd build such a house to live in.

Ciaran noticed an old robot standing at the corner of the garden and approached it. It hadn't been operated for a long time. If dust existed in Eudaiz, the machine must have gathered a lot of it. He activated the robot.

The machine came back to life. After humming for a second, it blinked and looked at Ciaran. At first, the monitor on its chest was blank. Then it seemed to reconnect to the current network, and it updated its system.

Text appeared on the monitor on the robot's chest. "Please verify your access."

Ciaran pressed his right palm to the control panel.

"Left palm please," the text stated.

Ciaran pressed his left palm to the control panel.

"Welcome to Sciphil Three's residence, Ciaran LeBlanc—king-to-be of Eudaiz," the robot verbalized.

"Is there a surveillance system in this garden? I need to know what happened here before I activated you," Ciaran said.

"Yes. The data is available in your control room," the robot said.

Ciaran nodded and turned to go to the house.

"Please accept my condolences about Bran's death. It was a great loss for Eudaiz," the robot said.

Ciaran paused and looked at the machine. "You are one smart robot."

"My name is Robert. I am the first-generation robot that could potentially handle data from the EYE."

Ciaran glanced around to ensure no one was close by. "I thought you were a garden robot."

"No. I am the central robot. 245.21YZ ago, Bran deactivated me here because he was in haste to leave for a mission."

"How long ago?" Ciaran asked, arching an eyebrow.

"My apologies. Converted into Earth time, it has been the equivalent of thirty-three years since he deactivated me."

"No one has reactivated you since then. How do you know your information is up-to-date?"

"Only a King Sciphil can activate me. You will be King Sciphil in twenty-eight days from now after your coronation. You will have access to the full data of the EYE. My system has been connected to the central databank. It is up-to-date."

Ciaran hissed audibly. He didn't know how much intelligence they had here. How much surveillance data would be available and to whom. Attempting to access the EYE system violated multiversal law and would result in a death penalty.

"We are not authorized to access data from the EYE system. I have no intention of building that databank. Neither did Bran," Ciaran stated as clearly as possible to the robot. He knew the message was being recorded.

"You do not have to worry about surveillance. No one in Eudaiz has the privilege to access King Sciphil's data in his private residence."

Ciaran smiled. *You're a robot. You're allowed to be naive,* he thought. "All right, Robert, how many others have lived in this residence?"

"Pierre LeBlanc until 1655. Aedan LeBlanc until 1755. Ealga LeBlanc until 1805. Malachi LeBlanc until 1976. Bran LeBlanc until 2015. Current owner, Ciaran LeBlanc," the robot narrated the information in a monotone voice.

But every word cut at him like a knife on bone. Generations of his family had been involved in this. And he hadn't known. His parents had worked their whole life to keep him out of it. To spare him the pain of power and responsibility to people he didn't know.

Ciaran LeBlanc, King of Eudaiz. Ciaran shook his head. He wasn't sure how long it would be before he got used to this life. A few months ago, he was a business man, running his family global pharmaceuticals empire out of his London headquarters.

Now he was here, working toward his kingship. There would be a lot to do before his coronation. If claiming the kingship of this universe was easy, there shouldn't have to be much bloodshed required.

He glanced around. Every brick in this place was soaked with the mystery of his family. The mysterious aura that had followed his family for generations. From Earth to the multiverse. Some people considered his family the most mysterious family on Earth.

Perhaps they were right.

He looked at his hands. There was blood on these hands. He'd killed to get here. But as Bran had said, it took a life to save a life. He didn't have to be a virtuous king—he only needed to be a just king.

But would he be capable of being a just king? What would it cost him to do the right thing for the citizens of this gigantic universe?

His emotions were his weakness. He was a human, not a robot. And when it came to his family, he would not compromise. Ever. He would do whatever it took to protect them. Everything else came second to that.

Family!

It dawned on him now why Madeline had fainted.

CHAPTER 4

Madeline was agitated. She needed to tell Ciaran about her precognition. But since Ciaran had found her in the garden, he and the others had made her lie down like a sick puppy. She protested. But then they'd taken a complicated-looking wristwatch off her, and the next thing she knew, she felt as weak as . . . a sick puppy.

At a corner of the room, Ayana Dee, Sciphil Two, and Pete Chandler, Sciphil Nine were talking. They had helped her and Ciaran a lot during the process of coming here. Ayana had been born in Eudaiz. She was as beautiful as an angel. Pete was a British man, recruited later in his life. He was like a kind uncle to Madeline.

Ciaran strode into the hall from a wing of connected corridors. His face was unfathomable—a typical Ciaran expression. He crouched next to her. "How are you feeling?" he asked.

"I'm perfectly fine. I'll feel better if they give me back that wrist unit."

Ciaran nodded toward Ayana, who was holding the wrist unit. She approached and gave the little machine back to Madeline. As soon as she put it on, waves of energy pumped into her body. She felt like a new person. She sat up, but she wasn't sure if she should tell Ciaran about the precognition in front of Ayana and Pete.

After all, she and Ciaran had just arrived in this universe. They didn't know who were friends and who were foes.

"I've taken a look around the residence. Everything looks fine. We can stay here. The top priority for us now is to plan Madeline's officiation as Sciphil One, am I right?" Ciaran asked.

Ayana answered, "Yes, indeed. It is important that she receives her full power in Tower One. Her succession had been authorized and lined up at the precise astronomical time, two days from now. If we fail to officiate her, the power of Tower One will fail—and so will Eudaiz."

"Understood," Ciaran said.

"Let me show you the map." Ayana turned on a floating screen, revealing a map of Eudaiz.

Eudaiz was organized in circles. The towers of power, clearly labeled, stood in a protected area. In the middle was Tower Three, the king tower. The other eight towers were located in a circle surrounding it. They looked like the eight petals of a sunflower.

Ayana pointed to the king tower and said, "This is the core of Eudaiz's power. It must be protected at all costs. The king has access to all towers. However, each Sciphil has access only to their own tower. So, Madeline, after officiation, you will have full access to Tower One. I have full access to Tower Two. And Pete has access to Tower Nine. Ciaran has access to all."

Madeline gestured widely. "So, given how important the towers are, security is critical. This universe has more than six hundred billion citizens. This must be a massive area. How can you guarantee security for the towers?"

Ayana smiled. "The tower zone is called the Sciphil zone. No citizens are allowed in there. The area is self-contained and quite small. The security of the Sciphil zone is strict and has never been breached in five hundred years. The towers have no entry point for anyone except the Sciphil of the tower and the king. Within each tower, there are nine round protective layers—they would spin and grind any unauthorized individuals into dust if they attempted to trespass."

Madeline nodded.

Pete pointed to a large circle which wrapping outside of the Sciphil zone. He said, "This is the Sciphil residential area. Each Sciphil has a residence, located as close to his or her respective tower as possible. We are here, at Sciphil Three residence." He pointed to a dotted line. "The internal capsule is strictly private and secure. It operates only for people with the right access. The capsule terminals are like subway systems in New York or London. So really, within the Sciphil zone and Sciphil residence areas, I wouldn't worry too much about security."

Ayana pointed to a larger circle outside the Sciphil residential area. "This is where the six hundred billion citizens live." The area took up a large area of the map. Ayana continued. "There are eight districts, located in circles in the outer ring here. Each Sciphil governs a district. No citizen has ever been allowed into the Sciphil zone."

"There are nine Sciphils and eight districts. Who doesn't have a district to govern?" Ciaran asked.

"You, Ciaran." Ayana smiled.

Pete laughed. "You have to manage all of the Sciphils and handle important matters such as protecting Eudaiz from our enemies. I think it's only fair to exempt you from the administrative duties of governing a district."

"From what I know, the Black Rock is our number one enemy. Is that information accurate?" Ciaran asked.

Pete shook his head. "No. It's speculative. That universe attacks us all the time because they don't have much energy or natural resources. Other universes may have attacked Eudaiz before, but not during the five hundred years' reign or our Sciphil council. There is no guarantee they won't attack us in the future."

"Have the Black Rock ever breached our security in the Sciphil zone?" Madeline asked.

"No," Ayana responded.

Ciaran nodded. "All right. It's been a long day. I think we should continue this discussion tomorrow."

"It feels as if a day here has fifty hours," Madeline said.

Pete smiled. "We don't use hours. A day here has nine units. Three for the morning, three for the afternoon, and three for the night. Each unit has one hundred slots. At the moment, it is the fiftieth slot of the night. The average person should have at least one unit of sleeping time a day."

Madeline rolled her eyes. Another set of rules and numbers to remember.

"Thank you, Pete. I'll be sure we get enough sleep." Ciaran smiled.

Pete nodded. "Especially you."

Ciaran arched an eyebrow.

Pete continued, "The battles you engaged in before arriving here have drained you of all of your natural energy. In Eudaiz, energy is everything. It's life. Eudqi is a special energy for Sciphils. It's like your blood. However, in your case, you won't receive full power until after your coronation. So right now, your energy is fragile and very temporary. Be sure you take advantage of the resting time so that your body can recharge what's used up during the day."

Ciaran raised a hand in frustration. "What you're saying is that, at the moment, I don't have the natural energy to operate my body. And I have to rely on the eudqi—like batteries?"

"Precisely," Pete smiled.

"So don't pick a fight," Madeline laughed.

"We'd better go to sleep now," Ciaran muttered.

"Not here, I hope," Ayana said.

"Why not?" Ciaran asked.

"This place has been vacant for more than thirty years. It can't be comfortable. Madeline has a fully operational Sciphil One residence. You both have full access," Ayana said.

"Yes, we'll go to Sciphil One residence later. But I'd like to have a bit of time here with Madeline, if we may," Ciaran said.

"It's only for one night. We can manage. If you could stop by again tomorrow and take us to Tower One, it would be greatly appreciated." Madeline smiled.

Ayana nodded. "Very well then. We will let you have some privacy. It's been a long day."

Ayana and Pete left the residence.

Madeline opened her mouth to tell Ciaran about what she had seen in the garden, but before she could say a word, Ciaran had locked his lips with hers. Whenever he engaged in such an intimate act, she was defenseless.

Suddenly, Ciaran glanced toward the side door. "Who's that?" he shouted and darted toward the door, weapon drawn.

CHAPTER 5

A short moment later, Ciaran came back in with a grin on his face and a remote control in his hand. "It was a flying surveillance camera. This entire place is serviced by robotic staff. No humans. You can do whatever you want here without anyone gawking . . ."

He continued to speak, but all she could focus on was her sinfully handsome husband. It didn't matter what he said now. He was safe and sound. That was all that mattered to her. She shuddered recalling the battles they had just been through to get to this universe.

She couldn't forget the warmth of his blood on her hands. She had been tormented by hopelessness when he was going down and she didn't know what to do.

But they had left those incidents in the past. And she hoped never to experience that feeling again.

She smiled at him when he said something about the use of technology. She really did mean to tell him about her precognition. But hell, her stomach quivered with lust every time he spoke. She could easily forget the universe and drown in the sight and sound of him.

She still didn't understand how he could possibly be hers. Called her biased, but her husband had to be the most gorgeous and intelligent man in the cosmos. Six foot three—or maybe even taller. His slender frame made his clothes or whatever he draped himself in look elegant. Beneath the material were the muscles that were disturbingly and distractingly beautiful.

His long, thick black hair almost touched his shoulders, framing the God-given face she loved. His intense gray eyes always seemed look straight into her soul. They twinkled when intrigued, and she loved it when they twinkled because of something she had said. His lips were made for kissing, and to that point, that was exactly what she wanted to do right now.

Ciaran paused at the expression on her face. Then he smiled, and his eyes twinkled. He approached the bench where she sat, brushed his thumb across the dimple on her left cheek.

"My first councillor, what's on your mind?" he asked and kissed her. Apparently, he didn't expect an answer.

As much as it embarrassed her, she couldn't help but let out an audible purr at his kiss and touches. The movement of his hands on her body was heavenly. He knew every curve on her body better than even she did, but he still traced them with his long fingers—those of an artist.

Perhaps he was an artist—an artist in lovemaking. He was so inventive that she couldn't keep up with him. Every time they made love, it was like the first time. But this was the first time they had been intimate in this strange universe.

She slid her hands underneath his shirt. He knew her body. She knew his. They gave. They took. They moved together in perfect rhythm. A brush of the lips. The heat of a tongue on bare skin. The pressure of fingertips on sensitive spots.

They knew it all.

They had done it all.

But each time, it was a new experience.

And they enjoyed it. Taking each other to the pinnacle of pleasure.

After a while, they lay still until she hopped up and propped herself up on her elbow, glancing around. "Where exactly *are* we?"

Ciaran chuckled. "I'd call this a broom closet. But with the lack of a broom or other cleaning tools, I'm guessing it's some kind of storage room. What it's storing, I have absolutely no idea."

He kissed her forehead and lifted her chin. "Why are you so reluctant to go to Sciphil One residence? It will be yours soon."

"I'm not staying with you? If my memory serves me correctly, I'm your wife—so I ought to be with you, staying here."

"In the broom closet?" he teased.

Madeline played with his hair. "Why are you so reluctant to stay *here?* It's yours now."

Ciaran fingered her dimple again and drew her into his arms. "I need more people around to take care of you." He kissed her cheek. "You're pregnant."

Madeline snorted. "If we keep up this broom closet activity, it will happen soon!"

"You're already carrying our twins, Madeline—a boy and a girl."

Madeline stared at her husband, speechless.

CHAPTER 6

Madeline whirled around, back and forth in the grand hall. She was sure all of the statues, marble columns, and arches were peering down at her, laughing at her confusion.

"You're making yourself dizzy, Madeline. You fainted in the garden before. I don't care for it to happen again," Ciaran said.

"I had a precognition in the garden. That was why I fainted."

"Why didn't you tell me?"

Madeline raised her arms in the air in frustration. "I didn't have a chance, Ciaran! Ayana and Pete were here. We talked about important stuff. Then you came in. Then there was the business in the broom closet. Then you dropped this information bomb on me!" She pointed at her tummy.

"I'm sorry. I know you're confused." He pulled her into his arms. "What did you see in your precognition?"

She frowned. She didn't know what was more important—her precognition or her pregnancy. "You said the machine detected that the children were conceived precisely during the Red Stage of the Daimon Gate? I mean, it's not like we have sex like rabbits, but we had a lot of it before the Daimon Gate tests."

Ciaran held back a laugh and nodded. "The EYE scanner detected and reported the information when I visited the Host of the Daimon Gate."

She looked at him. *That visit.* The emotion in his eyes was still so raw it stabbed at her heart. He hadn't had time to heal—if he would ever heal—from that emotional wound. To travel from Earth to Eudaiz and qualify as Sciphils, they'd had to pass the Daimon Gate tests—the most stringent, brutal, and nastiest tests in the cosmos.

She shuddered remembering them.

Ciaran had discovered how, when, and by whom he was conceived when they'd visited the Host residence in the Daimon Gate. Children conceived during the Red Stage of the Daimon Gate tests were the best beings in the cosmos. He was one of them. That explained his incredible talents and abilities.

Also, because of the desire to have such a special child, Ciaran wasn't conceived in love, but from a rape and brutal violence against his mother. Madeline knew how much it had hurt him to kill the man who gave him his life.

Justice for his mother.

For the integrity of the virtuous world in the Daimon Gate.

Whatever the reason, she knew it had hurt him to kill Bran as much as it would have if he hadn't killed the man. She knew he bemoaned the father he had never had. She could sense the unbearable pain he suffered, and she wished she could share the load. But he would never tell her about the pain. Sometimes he forgot she was psychic.

If their children had been conceived in the Red Stage of the Daimon Gate test, they would be just like him. They would be the best beings in the cosmos.

She sighed, thinking about the challenging period of motherhood ahead. She could barely operate a computer! How would she handle two freakishly smart kids? Not one. But two!

"Madeline!"

"Huh?"

"What did you see in your precognition?" Ciaran repeated his question.

"I saw words in blood on the wall saying *ENNEAD WILL KILL YOU ALL*. It might not mean anything." She snorted and rolled her eyes. "I'm pregnant. It could well be a hormonal issue!"

Ciaran smiled, but the smile didn't reach his eyes. "Ennead means a group of nine. It's mostly used in Egyptian mythology when referring to nine gods. Given that we have nine Sciphils and nine towers to protect, I don't think it's coincidental."

Madeline sighed. "Ciaran, sometimes it's nice when you don't know things."

He chuckled. "It's a curse, isn't it? Knowing too much."

"Owww," Madeline moaned. She winced and grabbed at her stomach.

"What's wrong?" Ciaran asked.

"Nothing. Just a cramp. Or a muscle spasm, maybe."

"Are you sure it's nothing?"

"If anything, it's because you told me I've been carrying twins for two days."

"The EYE system identified the precise time of conception."

"Right, so if there's that much surveillance around, they must have also recorded the smoking hot sex scene in the broom closet. Are you sure the data won't go viral on the internet—or whatever the Eudaizian equivalent is?" she asked. "Ow . . ." she cried again and clutched at her stomach. "This sucks."

She pressed her palm against the wall, breathing deeply. She remained still for a moment, waiting for the pain to settle. Puking in this grand hall didn't sound like a good idea. Madeline turned around and saw Ciaran's green face.

"Ciaran, if you look like that now, how are you going to handle it when we're deep in the throes of childbirth?"

Her husband—the know-it-all Ciaran, the best in the cosmos in pharmaceuticals and technology, the commander of his worlds on Earth and in Eudaiz—was obviously out of his element where her space pregnancy was concerned.

"Robert!" Ciaran shouted.

"Who?"

A robot of human size and shape scurried over in response to Madeline's question. "Yes, Ciaran?" the robot asked.

"Are there people other than robotic staff at in Sciphil One residence?"

"Yes. There are two Eudaizian staff members. English speaking. Highly skilled in administrative and domestic matters."

"All right, we are going to Sciphil One residence right now." When Ciaran donned his do-not-protest tone, Madeline simply nodded in agreement.

He slid his arms protectively around her waist and led her to the side door.

Suddenly, a chill ran up Madeline's spine. She glanced back at the grand hall and saw the words *Kyle Wolf* flashing in red blood on the wall. She blinked and looked again. The words had disappeared.

Her psychic mind told her the cold-blooded mind-bender had made it to Eudaiz. And she had a feeling they were heading toward another bloodbath. It was much too soon for her to engage in another battle.

And this time, it wouldn't be just another fight. She was carrying the citizens of a huge district on her shoulders–and twins in her tummy.

CHAPTER 7

Ciaran and Madeline entered an area that looked like a private train station. Madeline guessed the strange vehicle the size of a minibus and the shape of her vitamin pill was what they called a capsule, the key means of travel in Eudaiz. While Madeline gawked at the capsule, Ciaran entered and manned the capsule with ease—no more difficult than driving his sports cars on Earth.

Ciaran entered their destination of Sciphil One residence on the control panel. A robotic voice said, "Destination: Sciphil One residence. Trip duration:

five time slots. Gate security notification confirmed. Tunnel security check: one hundred percent."

Ciaran executed the trip. They barely felt the movement of the capsule. Madeline could tell they were moving based on the trip progress report and the percentage of completion displayed on a map on the screen.

Something suddenly hit the capsule, pushing it slightly aside. Ciaran pressed the assist button, but it didn't respond. He tried the red rescue system. It flashed once briefly, and then the entire system in the capsule died.

They felt another hit at their side. The wall of the capsule melted away, leaving a large hole. White smoke poured in.

Ciaran shoved at the door lever to open it. It wouldn't budge. He used his dagger to stab at the air cushion of the doorframe. He loosened it and pushed the door open. Ciaran and Madeline jumped out just before it shriveled into a pile of melted material.

A whirl of wind sucked the melted material toward the outside of the tunnel via a large hole. Ciaran and Madeline were pulled toward it by an incredible force. Ciaran grabbed the edge of the broken wall with one hand and held fast to

Madeline with the other. Her body hung halfway outside the tunnel, drawn by the vacuum of the atmosphere.

There was no breathable air on the other side of the tunnel, and Madeline drifted in and out of consciousness. She could no longer hang on to Ciaran. He pulled her inward—against the intense force of the suction—and swung her back inside the tunnel. He climbed back inside and carried Madeline away from the ominous hole.

A small spaceship then plugged itself into the hole, and six identical human-looking soldiers exited, charging at Ciaran with weapons similar to guns. Ciaran laid Madeline down on the floor and pulled his daggers. The creatures shot at him. His clothes were beam-proof, so the lasers that struck him bounced off his vest. Quick as lightning, he charged. In what seemed like no time at all, their body parts littered the floor of the tunnel, melting into black puddles and evaporating. Ciaran grabbed their guns.

Madeline had recovered after breathing in some inside air. She approached and grabbed two guns for herself.

"Are you okay to walk?" Ciaran asked.

She nodded.

"We should move quickly before something else comes."

They ran in the direction the capsule had been traveling before its meltdown. A rumbling sound echoed from the hole. Ciaran looked back and saw a dozen robotic soldiers—covered in steel and brandishing swords—closing in on them.

Ciaran and Madeline pulled their guns and fired. The guns caused absolutely no damage to the robots.

"Use the daggers. There are gaps in their armor between their necks and bodies and holes in the center of their breastplates," Ciaran said quickly. Madeline drew her daggers. Ciaran pushed her behind him, fighting and withdrawing at the same time.

Ciaran knew when he had the advantage in a fight—and when he didn't. This time, he knew they had no advantage. They were outnumbered. And these robots seemed smarter than those he had killed before. They focused on the weaker opponent—they were concentrating their attack on Madeline.

Ciaran took down three of them. The robots slashed at him. Their swords slashed through his protective vest.

One of them sliced at Madeline's left arm. Blood seeped out from her protective clothes, running down her forearm.

It dawned on him that he wouldn't be able to protect Madeline if the fight continued. He hadn't had time to plan. He didn't know anything about these creatures.

Mere fist fighting was a stupid move.

"That's enough," Ciaran said. He dropped his daggers and raised his hands in a surrendering gesture.

He held his breath. He didn't know if they understood English, but he figured his gesture of surrender was universal.

Or in this case, multiversal . . .

He could only hope.

CHAPTER 8

In a dark dungeon, under the flickering light of a small fire, Kyle tapped his bony fingers on the blade of a black sword. The contact didn't produce the sound of pure metal, but something darker, thicker, and more surreal. He narrowed his eyes and examined the sword carefully.

Kyle was not much into physical weapons. He preferred to use mind control. After all, it was his unique talent. But in dealing with the LeBlancs, he thought it prudent to gather all the weapons he could get his hands on. He would not lose a fight to Ciaran. Again.

He glanced at a human shaped creature standing nearby and waiting for his command. "Any news?" he asked the creature.

"Not yet, Master."

Kyle shook his head. He had been given the lowest ranked and most unskilled troops in the cosmos as punishment for his unsuccessful attempt to attack the LeBlancs on Earth.

"I've given them the precise route of their travel. How hard can it be, ambushing a small capsule of two people? They'd better not waste my hard-earned intelligence. I would have done it myself if they'd given me a bloody combat vehicle," Kyle snarled.

"I'm sorry, Master. It's outside my control."

"I'm not saying it's your fault, dumbass. Get out of my sight!" Kyle shouted.

The creature scurried out without glancing back.

***

In the tunnel, the robots stared at Ciaran's surrendering gesture. Then the one who appeared to be more senior nodded. They grabbed Ciaran and Madeline, pushed them toward the spaceship, and locked them in a small compartment.

Ciaran checked the gash on Madeline's arm.

"Your arm is bleeding, and you have a cut on your back, Ciaran."

He shook his head. "I'm fine. My injuries are minor, but yours aren't. They—"

"I'm pregnant, but I'm not crippled, Ciaran. Stop fussing."

Nodding, he flopped down on the bench next to Madeline. She could see fatigue clouding his beautiful eyes. She was cold—her teeth chattered, and her body shook. Ciaran pulled her into his arms and held her, hoping he could give some warmth and comfort. It didn't seem to help.

The door of the compartment slid open, and a man who appeared to be in his forties entered.

"Ciaran LeBlanc, King of Eudaiz," the monotone voice filtered through a robotic translator, "we will take you to our central—"

"I need you to increase the temperature in this compartment and give me the necessary medical equipment to tend to her injury," Ciaran interrupted, pointing at Madeline's arm.

"I am not authorized to change the specifications of the vessel. I need you to—"

"We won't go anywhere or do anything until you do as I ask."

Madeline was fading quickly. She couldn't handle the environment outside the Sciphil zone. Ciaran knew he wasn't going to get anywhere quickly with this robot in human form.

A loud bang echoed in from the side of the spaceship.

Electronic sparks and smoke fumes spread through the corridor, distracting the robotic man. Ciaran grabbed him and snapped his neck with one twist. Bunches of wires poked out of the broken neck, and smoke swirled from the eye sockets. Ciaran grabbed the robot's gun.

He helped Madeline out of the compartment. She could walk, but Ciaran scooped her up and hurried through the long corridor. Via a broken wall, Ciaran saw very small capsule shooting at the spaceship. He didn't know who piloted it.

From the far end of the corridor, robots ran toward him.

Carrying Madeline in his arms, Ciaran strode quickly toward the hole in the wall of the spaceship. The suction was strong and was drawing Ciaran and Madeline out. He held his stance to resist it.

The robots on this ship were fast approaching. He could put Madeline down and shoot at them. But how long could he hold on to this fight? He didn't know how many of them were on the ship or how long his gun would last.

He took a gun from a rookie robot. The weapon couldn't be too advanced.

The air pumping through the hole on the ship wall was too thin. Madeline was completely out of it now.

The small capsule outside hovered and opened its wing door. It was waiting for Ciaran to leap over to it. This wasn't exactly a safe tarmac. If he couldn't make the jump, only God knew what was underneath.

He looked at the approaching robots again. They charged at them, but they didn't shoot. He frowned. Whoever wanted them must want them captured alive. And who was manning the small capsule over there? Were they friends or foes?

Hell. He glanced back at the robots again then stepped back to gain some space. He ran fast with

Madeline in his arms and leaped toward the small door of the other vehicle.

CHAPTER 9

Kyle swung his black sword. The head of the creature rolled on the concrete floor like a soccer ball. He knew there was no point killing a messenger. He just wanted to test his weapon.

His intelligence was wasted. It didn't surprise him as much as he had anticipated. Coming back to Eudaiz and fighting himself back to power shouldn't be easy. If it wasn't challenging, it wouldn't be exciting.

Kyle smirked to himself. He had plans. Good ones. Maybe an adjustment he would make was to not rely on supplies from the Black Rock. If that universe had ever come close to taking over Eudaiz, they would have done it a long time ago.

Why waste time on an insider like him?

Kyle looked at the black liquid from the creature on the blade of his sword. This creature was from somewhere else, not from the Black Rock. Its body wouldn't evaporate into thin air. Kyle sighed. That meant he had to do some housecleaning. Damn inconvenient.

***

The rough landing in the small capsule jolted Madeline awake. She found herself on the floor, and Ciaran loomed over her.

"There you are. How are you feeling?" he asked.

She was sure she was getting better than he was. She could feel she was gaining energy while he was losing it. She couldn't move yet, but she would very soon. Ciaran scooped her off the floor and put her on a comfortable chair.

There, she saw the person who was manning the capsule, and her stomach fluttered.

The woman was stunning. As to why her stomach protested, she had no idea. Maybe it wasn't the sight of the woman but Ciaran's appearance. Dark circles had formed under his eyes. He'd lost a lot of blood. She could feel the energy leaking out of him in waves.

Not only that, the energy he was using wasn't his. As Pete had said this morning, her energy was natural. She could recharge at the same time as she was using it. But his was totally artificial and could only be charged when he rested.

While Ciaran checked on her injuries, the attractive woman turned around. Sensing the look from the woman, Ciaran turned back to face her.

Everything about the woman's appearance was perfect. She looked to be just about six feet tall. Striking blue hair, deep blue eyes, and milky skin.

"My name is Sizx. I am the head of Eudaiz's intelligence system based in Alphi. I know you are Ciaran and Madeline LeBlanc. When the system alert came, it was too late to route the data and call for proper assistance, so I took the liberty of rescuing you in my private vehicle. I hope you don't mind."

Madeline saw a flash of admiration cross Ciaran's eyes. And to her astonishment, she swore she saw them twinkle.

"On the contrary, thank you for the rescue. Could you take us to Sciphil One residence?" Ciaran asked.

"We are now outside the Sciphil's zone. The direct way is dangerous and is now being blocked by the attackers. We will have to go outside the Eudaiz secured zone and enter via District Seven."

"How dangerous is that?" Ciaran asked.

"I don't know. I've never done it before."

"Any alternatives?"

"Not many. District Seven is the shortest route. My capsule took a couple of hits. The communication system has been paralyzed. I don't know how to fix it."

Ciaran crouched next to Madeline's chair, checking her temperature and her pulse. "Can you hang on?"

She nodded. She would move again very soon. Goddamnit. She hated being useless.

"Is the capsule in hovering mode?" Ciaran asked.

Sizx nodded. Ciaran approached and adjusted something on the control panel. "Who attacked us?" Ciaran asked Sizx while he worked.

"In theory, I'd say it was the Black Rock robots. But I've never seen robots like the ones that came off that ship."

"If they attack us again outside of the Eudaiz secured zone, what do we have to protect ourselves?" Ciaran asked.

Sizx shook her head, her magnificent blue hair dancing on the shoulders of her perfect body. "We have nothing. I told you—this is my private capsule. The self- defense mechanism used up all of its ammunition shooting at the spaceship. It isn't designed for combat."

"It was suicidal to engage in combat with that spaceship, Sizx. Why did you do it?"

Sizx turned. "I was on my way to Central Intelligence to prepare for your coronation when I got a faint rescue signal. I knew your system was dead, and you wouldn't be getting help any time soon. I'm a Eudaizian citizen—and your head of intelligence. It's my duty to protect you."

"I'm grateful. You're very brave, Sizx," Ciaran said.

Madeline could see Ciaran was drifting off. His eyes glazed over. She lifted her shoulder and figured that she could move her left hand.

"Ciaran!" Sizx called out.

Ciaran snapped back to consciousness. "I beg your pardon. What did you just say?" he asked.

"When did you last have your one unit of sleep? You don't have your wrist unit with you, so I can't check your energy level."

Ciaran shook his head as if he couldn't understand what Sizx was saying. He looked at Madeline.

Madeline flexed her muscles and could feel her right shoulder now. "He must have lost his wrist unit during the fight. And he hasn't had any sleep units since we arrived," Madeline said and tried to move her legs.

Ciaran shook his head, trying to stay alert without much success.

"Your system will shut down if you don't take the resting time. If you want to stay awake, then you will have to manually increase the energy level," Sizx said.

"How?" Ciaran asked.

Sizx put a square patch of something that looked like a black Band-Aid on the dashboard. "This will give you nine units straight."

"No, I won't take anything." Ciaran shook his head and staggered back.

"Take this, or you have to rest." Six advanced, holding the patch in her hand.

"I can't . . ."

Ciaran fell over onto Sizx as his system shut down. He was totally out of it. Sizx lowered him to the floor.

"Could you patch up his injuries before waking him?" Madeline asked, trying harder to move her useless legs.

Sizx nodded at Madeline's request. She quickly grabbed a medical kit from a small compartment by the control panel. She secured the gashes on Ciaran's arm and back then peeled off the energy patch and stuck it to the inside of Ciaran's left wrist.

In a short moment, Ciaran winced and opened his eyes.

Then he jumped to his feet, shoving Sizx against the dashboard and sending tools and equipment crashing on his way. Sizx pushed her hand accidentally on a control button as she caught her balance. The capsule shuddered, swiveled, and dipped.

CHAPTER 10

Ayana stormed into the control room at her Sciphil Two residence. Fear stabbed at her. She had just left Ciaran and Madeline at Sciphil Three residence earlier in the night. Now her wrist unit flared in red alarm. Ciaran's private capsule had been attacked en route to Sciphil One residence.

This had not happened in five hundred years.

Her fear was an inexplicable emotion. She was eighty percent Eudaizian. She was supposed to be in complete control of her emotions. Expression of them was a sign of weakness for a Eudaizian leader.

She couldn't afford that. She was the second in charge in the Sciphil council after the king.

She was still trying to accept the fact that Ciaran was Bran's biological son. For the short time Bran had ruled as the king, she had learned so much from him. She admired him. And she'd never understood why he didn't have a family—a son to succeed him. Rather, he had recruited Ciaran as a child from Earth.

Now she understood. Although he had never been told of their relation, Bran had always sensed a connection with Ciaran.

Then Bran came back into her life after having been missing thirty-three years. But they hadn't had a chance to have a proper conversation before he died. She'd lost him forever.

And now she couldn't protect the only thing he'd left behind—his only son.

"Ayana, central hasn't responded yet. We have no trace of what took them." The image of Pete came across the screen, concern blanketing his face.

"I'm going down to the tunnel," Ayana said.

"No. It's been damaged. We have to wait for central backup."

"Ciaran and Madeline are on their own, Pete. No guards and no technology to support them. I can't let anything happen to them."

"But we have to wait for guards from central. Our residential guards aren't trained for the outer zone where their capsule was attacked."

"I'm taking my men and will go to the tunnel. You're in charge now should anything happen to me. Understood?"

"N—"

"That will be all, Pete. Thank you." Ayana turned off the communicator before Pete could say anything more.

***

The capsule seemed to settle after the big spin.

"What did you do to me?" Ciaran pressed Sizx against the control panel.

From behind him, Madeline approached. "She was just trying to help, Ciaran."

He turned around and saw Madeline had recovered from her injury. It must be something in the Eudaizian air. It seemed as if she could absorb its energy and process it.

Apparently he couldn't do it because he didn't have any natural energy left to kick-start the process. But his injuries were healing now. And he felt strong.

Ciaran released Sizx. Then he noticed that the wound on his arm had been tended to, and he saw the energy patch on his wrist. "I'm sorry," Ciaran said and reached for the energy patch to peel it off.

"Don't. It will keep you energized for nine units without resting. You said you wanted to take Madeline to Sciphil One residence. That borrowed energy is the only thing that keeps you standing now," Sizx said.

Ciaran nodded. "Thank you. I'll return it." Then he turned toward Madeline. "How are you feeling?"

She grinned. "Like a superwoman."

The impact of something hitting the capsule knocked everyone off balance. Sizx scrambled up to look at the scanner. "I don't know how to handle this, Ciaran. We don't have any more ammunition."

"Where are we?" Ciaran asked her.

"Very close to District Seven. Right at the outskirts, I'd guess. The scanner has been damaged."

Another hit jostled the craft.

"Can we go outside? Abandon ship somehow?" Madeline asked.

"I'm not sure."

"Increase our speed?" Ciaran asked.

Another hit on the side of the capsule.

"Maybe . . ."

Ciaran did not wait for a response. He headed to the control panel. It couldn't be any harder than piloting a chopper. He knew how to do this. But the entire scanning system was down. They were flying blind in the sky—if there was a sky.

A hard hit came from another direction, throwing Madeline and Sizx to the floor. Ciaran retained his position by hanging on to the control panel.

"I'm so sorry. I don't know where we're heading now. The radar is broken," Sizx said.

Ciaran pushed the capsule up and then let it dive deep. He hoped if he dodged enough, they'd avoid being a further target. "Do we have a fuel indicator, Sizx?" he asked.

"No, we run on energy. The capsule was fully charged—it can last several days under normal conditions."

"Let me try to help. We are going to District Seven, right?" Madeline asked.

"You have another map, Madeline?" Sizx asked.

"I can track minds. Anyone in District Seven that we would know? I'm trying to get my bearings," Madeline asked.

Ciaran shook his head.

"What's the closest district to Seven that's in the same direction?" Ciaran asked.

"Nine. District Nine is the closest," Sizx said.

Madeline nodded. "That will work. I know Pete Chandler, Sciphil Nine." She closed her eyes to gather her concentration.

Sizx was baffled. She looked at Ciaran for an explanation.

"She's our walking-talking radar." Ciaran smiled.

Madeline said, "Turn right, Ciaran, and then go straight." Ciaran turned the capsule right without question. They flew a bit longer, and then the capsule began to descend rapidly.

"Out of energy," Sizx said. "We have to land."

Ciaran manned the capsule, landed quickly, and opened the door. From inside, they could see a gigantic wall about fifty feet away.

"That's a district boundary, but I'm not sure which one. As long as we can enter the gate, we should be fine."

Sizx stuck her head outside and looked around. She nodded to Ciaran and Madeline, signaling that the surrounding areas were safe.

"I'll verify and open the gate. Can you run straight from here to the gate?"

Ciaran glanced outside. The distance was about fifty feet. They should be fine running without breathing. It looked as if there was some gravity in effect. "Are you okay with that?" he asked Madeline. She nodded.

Sizx approached the thick wall and verified her right palm print on the control panel mounted there. A heavy gate slid open. She held it and signaled for Ciaran and Madeline to run. They charged from the capsule and headed for the gate.

From the corner of his eyes, Ciaran saw the shadows of three creatures. "Be careful," he yelled at Sizx, but it was too late.

The claw of a crab-like creature slashed at her. She fell but held fast to the panel to keep the gate open. Ciaran pushed Madeline through then pulled out his gun and shot at the creatures. They exploded and melted into a thick black substance that quickly vaporized.

Ciaran gathered Sizx up into his arms and dove through the gate just before it closed.

CHAPTER 11

A blast of wind and dark energy blew Ayana several feet and sent her rolling on the concrete floor of the broken tunnel. She shot back up to her feet and drew her Sciphil sword. Around her, her guards were dead. Most of their heads had exploded as they couldn't handle the frequency embedded in the dark energy.

From the shadows, Kyle walked out. "You have to admit that was impressive."

"Kyle, you have no place in Eudaiz. I give you one last chance to leave. Go and stay with the Black Rock."

"Now, why would I do that?"

"Your last opportunity has lapsed," Ayana said as she swung her sword and charged at him. Kyle raised his black sword and blocked her blow. He staggered back.

"You have to admit *that* was impressive," Ayana said and smiled graciously. "I know you weren't the one who took Ciaran and Madeline. Otherwise, you wouldn't be here."

Kyle ignored Ayana and frowned at his sword.

"If you expect that piece of scrap metal to go head to head against a Sciphil sword, then you are mistaken."

Kyle shook his head as if disappointed at his weapon. Ayana knew that without it, he couldn't fight against her. His energy had always been inferior to hers even when he was still acting as a Sciphil. But after Bran exiled him, he shouldn't have a drop of Eudaizian energy left.

Kyle looked at her now and said, "You're right. This weapon is inferior. But my intelligence is not. Let me tell you something. I don't know where Ciaran and Madeline are right now. But I can get the information easily. Because my mole is in your very council. How's that for a tip of the day?"

Kyle smirked, turned on his heel, and jumped across dimensions, vanishing in front of Ayana. She charged toward the dimensional gate, but she traveled too fast, not anticipating Kyle's return swing.

Another blast of dark energy hurled her smashing into the wall of the tunnel. She tumbled out of the hole on the wall. When she climbed back in, Kyle had gone.

***

Inside the gate, they stood at the edge of what looked like a forest. Sizx lay down on the soft grass, gasping for air.

"Sizx, please tell me what to do. I'm not going to let you die," Ciaran said.

She couldn't speak. Her hands clutched at the wound in her abdomen. Dark red blood poured out, soaking her blue vest.

Ciaran picked her up. "Where can I find help? Tell me, Sizx."

In front of them was a wide meadow, and they could see houses far off in the distance. Sizx signaled Ciaran to put her down, and she leaned against a tree.

"Give me the energy patch. I'll go and get help. You don't speak Eudaizian," Sizx said.

"It doesn't look like you can walk very far by yourself," Madeline said.

"I'm losing energy . . ."

"If I'm out of it when I remove the energy patch, is it safe for Madeline to be here by herself?" Ciaran asked.

"I can protect you, Ciaran," Madeline protested.

"Let's be realistic . . ." Ciaran growled.

"This is District Seven . . . The citizens are harmless, but I don't know what else is here. Black Rock creatures can disguise themselves in many forms. I need to go to seek help . . ." Sizx was fading. Her voice was barely audible.

Ciaran shook his head. "I can't use your reserved energy. Here it is." Ciaran pulled the patch from his left wrist. He swayed immediately. Sizx stuck her right wrist out, and he slapped the patch on.

Then he collapsed to the ground.

Madeline hurried to Ciaran's side. "Oh my God!" She remembered what Pete had said about Ciaran having no natural energy and having to rely on his eudqi, but she had no idea he could totally stop functioning like this.

Sizx recovered instantly with the patch. Her wound was still bleeding, but she could move quickly. She turned Ciaran around, sat him up, and rested him against the tree.

"He's fine. He needs this resting period, especially after borrowing heavily from my reserved energy."

"You call this resting? He looks half dead."

Sizx smiled briefly but then erased it from her face. "He'll be fine after some rest. I've never seen anyone rely so much on artificial energy. He looks as if there's nothing left in him. I'll go find help. You make sure Ciaran rests fully."

This woman didn't seem to understand that Ciaran was her husband, and she would do whatever it took to protect him. "Of course, I will," Madeline replied.

"One more thing," Sizx said. "I'd trust no one in the council if I were you. Don't try to call or contact anyone before I get back with some help. The fact that you and Ciaran are out here—vulnerable— rather than within the protective area suggests that someone at the top level of the council doesn't approve of the two of you. My prediction is that they want to take Ciaran down before the coronation has a chance to occur."

"Who will gain most if Ciaran doesn't come into power?"

Sizx shrugged. "I have no idea. I don't play those head games. I'll accept Ciaran as king. And as long as I'm on duty, I'll do my best to protect him. Remember—no communication, no verification, and trust no one while I'm gone. The Black Rock creatures can take all forms."

Then, in front of astonished Madeline, Sizx bent down and kissed Ciaran on the lips before she strode away.

Madeline was positive her jaw dropped. That blue-haired woman just kissed her husband! On the lips. She was sure that wasn't Eudaiz's everyday etiquette. It was totally unacceptable.

She sat down next to Ciaran and pulled him so that his head lolled on her shoulder. "See, I'm protecting you," Madeline cooed.

Long moments passed. Madeline checked her weapon several times, although she knew it was still there. She shifted, feeling the weight of Ciaran's body leaning against her. He was so out of it—so totally dependent on her. But if someone or something attacked them now, there wasn't much she could do.

She prayed to God again and cursed. God did not exist in Eudaiz. Madeline remembered when they had fought at Ciaran's house at Henley-on-Thames in England, when things had gone really bad and Ciaran was in serious trouble, she had promised God she would name her son after him if he helped them.

She tried to calm her nerves by thinking of names for her children now.

Sizx had been gone for a while, and Ciaran had not awakened. Madeline ran through the names for her son again.

She turned and kissed Ciaran on the cheek. He didn't stir.

Then she heard a noise that seemed to come from a nearby bush.

"Oh, no." If they were attacked right then, she didn't know what she would do. She wasn't sure if she could protect Ciaran.

Her body tensed, alarms going off in her head. "No, no. Come on." She looked at the rustling grass. "Let it be a rabbit," she muttered. "Dear God, I'm working on the name for my son right now. Please let it be a rabbit!"

The grass moved more violently. Someone or something was clearly running through it. And it couldn't possibly be a rabbit.

CHAPTER 12

Ralph Durant, Sciphil Seven, a formidable looking Caucasian in his mid-fifties, snarled at the blank screen in front of him. "I can't talk to a blank screen. We will resume the conversation when you fix the bloody technology."

The control room at Tower Seven was filled with computer monitors. A voice came out from the speaker through a great deal of static.

"This is a call from central, and it's urgent, sir. We haven't been able to locate king Sciphil, Ciaran LeBlanc, and Sciphil One, Madeline LeBlanc."

"Yes, I know. I've heard. What's new?"

"Could you please confirm if they have entered your district?"

"No. I told you. They're not at my residence."

"They might have gone out wider, sir. We need to know if they have entered your civilian areas."

"Do you know how many million citizens there are in District Seven?" Ralph snarled.

"We're talking about the safety of the king and Sciphil One, sir. Please cooperate with central."

Ralph mumbled some profanity and switched on his computer system. He glanced through a sea of data flowing through his screen. Then he frowned and hit the pause button. "What have we here?" he muttered.

He straightened up and talked to the blank screen.

"It looks like they've entered Gate 1. I'll go and pick them up."

"Thank you, sir."

The communicator went off-line. Ralph tucked his Sciphil sword into his belt and left the room.

At the other end of the line, Kyle wiped his bloody sword on the jacket of a dead technician. He glanced around and then opened a cabinet on the wall and shoved the dead body inside.

***

On the outskirts of District Seven, Madeline leaned Ciaran against the tree trunk and sprang to her feet. She stared apprehensively at the tall, moving grass.

From the grass, a few wild animals that look like rabbits stormed out, chased by a girl. Seeing Madeline, the girl ceased her chase. She stood still and observed Madeline with curiosity. The girl was about seven or eight and as beautiful as a little angel. She held a bunch of wildflowers in her hand.

Madeline smiled. The girl looked harmless—but Sizx had said that Black Rock spies could take any form.

The girl approached and smiled back at Madeline.

"Hello there." Madeline tried to be as friendly as possible.

A stream of melodious Eudaizian that sounded like a song poured out of the small child's mouth. Then she looked at Ciaran.

"He's just sleeping. He's very tired." Madeline smiled again, unsure how to handle the situation.

The girl pushed the flowers into Madeline's hand. Before Madeline could protest, she gave Madeline a peck on the cheek, and then she ran away.

Madeline released her held breath. At least the encounter had been quick and uneventful—but maybe it was too soon to draw conclusions. The girl returned with three adults. Madeline leaned Ciaran back onto the tree trunk and checked that her weapon was at ready.

The three adults approached.

Seriously . . . I don't speak Eudaizian, Madeline thought to herself.

The adults greeted Madeline politely. *What beautiful people,* Madeline thought. The Eudaizians looked at Ciaran, showing concern.

"No, no, don't worry about him. He's fine. He's just resting." Madeline spoke loudly and clearly but then realized that if they didn't understand her, there was no point in raising her voice—they weren't deaf.

Two more adults came with a stretcher.

"Oh, no, no. That's not necessary. We came from there." Madeline waved her arms frantically, pointing toward the gate they had recently entered. "We're waiting for a friend."

The man in his late sixties looked toward the gate and then spoke in English, "You must have come from Sciphil Central?"

Madeline remembered what Sizx had said. No verification.

"We were on our way to visit a friend. Our capsule broke down outside the gate. Our friend went to get help. So thank you for your concern, but we're fine."

Years in journalism had taught Madeline how to get information out of people—including those expert in avoiding questions. She was now applying her techniques, answering questions without giving out information.

The old man spoke calmly, "The air here is very thin. It will take him a long time to recover. You should come to our house. It's nearby, and we have credited air."

Madeline had no idea what credited air was. Her sixth sense told her that this family's concern for Ciaran's well-being was genuine. She knew she shouldn't trust anyone, but she couldn't bring herself to draw her weapon against these people. She started to wave the man with the stretcher off when she felt the dagger at her side move. The little girl had pulled it out to look at it.

"Oh no, sweetie. It's not a toy." Madeline grabbed the dagger, but not before the girl ran her fingertip across the blade.

A drop of blood welled in front of the girl's shocked eyes. She held up her finger, looked at the old man, and started to cry. The old man embraced the girl, saying something soothing in Eudaizian. Tears rolled down the girl's face.

A searing pain shot through Madeline's body. She grabbed her stomach. *Not now, not again,* she thought. She pressed her palm against the tree and breathed deeply.

Seeing Madeline in distress, the young girl left the man to approach her and pull at her hand. She wiped her tears and put on a grin. She said something that Madeline didn't need to know the language to understand—she wanted Madeline to feel better.

Madeline still leaned against the tree, trying to calm her twins down. Her tummy wasn't yet swollen. In fact, there was no sign of the pregnancy at all. If she didn't share her secret, nobody would know. For God's sake, the twins were only three days old. They shouldn't be causing her this much pain.

But the pain was unbearable. Madeline didn't know what to do, so she hugged the tree tightly, wishing the agony away.

The little girl pulled Madeline against her body and hugged her. Madeline embraced the girl, combing her fingers through her long, soft hair. A wave of comfort washed over her, and she felt an accompanying tingling sensation throughout her body.

Her pain was alleviated immediately.

She turned around and saw the other two men loading Ciaran onto the stretcher. She didn't know how to handle these nice people. She wished Ciaran would wake—he was always much better than she was in situations like this.

She didn't react quickly enough when the old man pulled out a portable device of some kind and pressed Ciaran's right palm against it.

He was verifying Ciaran's palm. He would find out who he was.

Sizx had told her—no conversation, no verification, and trust no one.

"No!!!" Madeline squealed for them to stop, but it was too late.

CHAPTER 13

The sight of Sizx returning to the meadow was like seeing a guardian angel. Madeline darted to Sizx, frantically pointing toward the men with the stretcher. Sizx seemed confused, and Madeline said between her teeth, "They verified him."

The old man looked at the monitor and looked at Madeline, confused.

Then Madeline realized with relief that they had tried to verify Ciaran's right palm, and they'd gotten no reading. He was the king—his verification came from his left palm. She strode toward them at once, attempting to stop them before they tried the verification again.

"We'd like to check his energy level, but our device is broken. I'm sorry. We should take him inside," the old man said.

Madeline pointed at Sizx. "Here's my friend." Then she said to Sizx, "Please tell them we can't go with them, Sizx."

"They're citizens here," said Sizx. "They're harmless. Plus, Ciaran will benefit from their credited air."

Madeline still didn't get the whole credited air thing, but she let it go, drawing in some *uncredited* air to calm herself down.

Sizx took the portable device from the man and pressed her right palm onto it. It verified her, and the group of Eudaizians respectfully stepped back. She instructed them to take Ciaran away. The old man pointed to his device, said something in Eudaizian, and pointed to Ciaran. Sizx made a dismissive gesture and returned to Madeline.

Madeline picked up the little girl. She said something, and Sizx translated. "She said she can walk by herself. She didn't want to hurt you before, and she's sorry."

Madeline put the girl down. "You didn't hurt me. You're so brave. Thank you so much for your help."

The girl smiled. Madeline pointed to herself. "I'm Madeline."

"I'm Gaia," the girl said in English. Madeline was astonished. Sizx raised an eyebrow.

"I'm Sizx. Nice to meet you, Gaia."

Gaia processed the information for a short moment and nodded. Sizx smiled. The old man approached, speaking English this time. "I'm Niw Hance, Gaia's grandfather. She loves to learn English."

"Very nice to meet you, Mr. Hance," Madeline said.

"Niw, please."

"Do you want Gaia to work for the Sciphils?" Sizx asked.

"It's up to her. Her father, Liam, can speak English well. But he likes to work here, not at Sciphil Central."

"What does he do?" Madeline asked.

"He's a medical doctor."

"Do people here get sick often? I heard you have a very pure environment compared to where I'm from," Madeline said.

"Where are you from?" Niw asked Madeline.

Sizx cleared her throat, communicating that Niw shouldn't have asked that question.

Niw grinned. "No, people don't get sick here. Medical facilities are used mostly for accidents, misuse of energy, or childbirth. Liam deals with research and development."

They turned into a small, charming town—looking surprisingly like any sleepy town in England—and stopped in front of a modern-looking house. Niw pressed his palm on a control panel, and the door slid open.

Madeline felt the difference in air quality as soon as she walked into the front hallway of the house. It was liked stepping into an air-conditioned room from a burning desert.

"We have a guest resting chamber. We'll put him in there," Niw said.

Madeline nodded.

Niw instructed two men to take Ciaran into the resting chamber. The living room—or whatever they called it here—had comfortable furniture and a screen in the corner. It seemed like a room in any ordinary household Madeline had seen on Earth.

"What's the deal with credited air?" Madeline asked Sizx.

"When people contribute something of value, they are rewarded with air credits."

"So it's like money?"

Sizx nodded. "It's an equivalent to your currency system. But don't speak to civilians about it. They wouldn't understand you. It's not a language barrier, but rather a societal structure. It's very different here compared to Earth."

"You seem to know an awful lot compared to the average person," Madeline commented.

"Well, I'm not an average person. I am educated because of my position in the intelligence system."

"Are you saying that average people in Eudaiz don't have access to education?"

"You're putting too much of a negative spin on it, Madeline. Education is not a privilege in Eudaiz. It gives people knowledge and artificial skills. It does not necessarily nourish people's natural talent. The only way to be happy is to live by your natural talent. If knowledge does not line up with your talent, it will cause unhappiness, and you won't find a place in Eudaiz."

"Well, without education, people can't get jobs. Will this still make them happy?"

"Sciphils provide everything to the citizens of Eudaiz for free. People earn credits for their contributions because they want to give back. They want to contribute by creating value using their natural talents. If they don't want to do anything, they don't have to."

"So why in this super-nice society with super-nice people are there folks who want to kill Ciaran before his coronation? What will his death give them?"

"You're talking about Sciphils. Except for Sciphil Four, Kyle Wolf, all Sciphils are human. They're more complicated."

The name Kyle Wolf hit her like a blast of icy water in the face. Madeline narrowed her eyes. "You're saying Kyle Wolf *isn't* complicated?"

Sizx shook her head. "He might be. He was exiled before my time, so I don't know."

The pain in her tummy started to throb again. Her vision began to waver. Madeline grabbed at the bookshelf for purchase.

"Ladies." Ciaran's voice came from the doorway.

Madeline drew in a breath and turned around to see her husband. She pasted a smile on her face and approached him. She played with the lapel of his shirt. "Well, I can see you're fully charged now, warrior."

Ciaran smiled. He rubbed his thumb on Madeline's left cheek then pulled her into his arms. She loved the feel of his heartbeat and her body pressed against his.

"How are you, Sizx?" Ciaran asked.

"Very well, thank you. I've arranged a capsule with a friend of mine. We can leave when you're ready."

"What I meant was how is your injury healing?" Ciaran asked.

Sizx looked to the floor for a brief moment to wash away any expression on her face. Then she looked up. "It's been tended to. Thank you for asking."

Ciaran raised Madeline's chin. "Your temperature has increased." The smile had disappeared from his face.

Madeline shrugged and tried to ignore the pain. "No, it's fine."

Sizx approached Madeline. Without saying a word, she grabbed Madeline's arm and snapped a device at it. It felt like a gunshot.

"What the hell was that?" Madeline asked angrily.

"Temperature double the normal range," Sizx said dryly, looking at her device. "What's your injury? You've been rubbing your abdomen all afternoon."

Alarm bells rang in Madeline's head. "Nothing. I don't have an injury." She withdrew, stepping away from Ciaran. Sensing something was going wrong, she scanned the room frantically for a way out.

"Madeline!" Ciaran approached and held her shoulders. "Tell me what's wrong, darling." He pulled her into his arms again. "Please. We'll get through this together. If you don't tell me what's wrong, I won't know what to do to help you!"

She couldn't tell him the babies were hurting her. A tear rolled down Madeline's face. Ciaran's eyes darkened as he saw the tear and her pain. He turned toward Sizx.

"My wife is pregnant. Does it normally hurt so much here? On Earth, it only hurts if something is wrong."

"How long has she been pregnant?" Sizx asked.

"Three days. What's the normal gestational period here?" Ciaran asked.

"Twenty-eight days," Sizx said.

"What? That's ridiculous." Madeline was astonished.

"The baby is full-term in twenty-eight days. The terms are divided into four seven-day stages. Within the first seven days, the baby should be positioned in the birth chamber," Sizx said.

"What the hell does that mean? You want to rip my children out and put them into alien tubes?" Madeline roared.

"It's . . . it's how it's . . ." Sizx stuttered out an explanation.

"What happens if the mother carries the baby full-term inside her body? Would it harm the mother?" Ciaran asked.

"I don't know," Sizx said.

"Get away from me." Madeline shrugged of Ciaran's hand, shoved Sizx, and tried to run to the door. But Ciaran grabbed her again.

Hearing the commotion, Niw and Gaia came out to the living room. Gaia's eyes widened when she saw Ciaran. Then she saw that Madeline was in tears.

"What happened?" Niw asked.

Ciaran figured that Gaia and Niw were related and that Niw was a man with a family.

"My wife is pregnant. Can you tell me what will happen if she carries the baby full-term?" he asked while holding tight to a wriggling Madeline.

Niw's eyes were huge. "Your voice! I recognize it! You must be related to Bran. You're royal. You . . . you ought to be our king."

"Niw," Sizx warned.

Niw backed off when he realized he was approaching Ciaran.

"Madeline is in a lot of pain. Please tell me, Niw, what will happen if a mother carries the baby in her body full-term?" Ciaran repeated.

Niw gathered himself together and cleared his throat. "If the baby remains inside the mother in seven days, the pain will be fatal." Niw grabbed at Gaia as if the little girl could help calm him.

"Then I won't let that happen." Ciaran kept his voice low. His eyes were so intense they made Gaia squirm. Madeline struggled more but couldn't break free of Ciaran's hold.

"Let me go, Ciaran. If anything happens to the children, I will never forgive you." The pain intensified so much she couldn't breathe properly. A mixture of sweat and tears streamed down her face.

"I can't lose you, Madeline," Ciaran growled.

"This is abortion, and I won't accept it!" Madeline screamed and struggled harder. She kicked her legs, pulled at Ciaran's shirt, punched his chest. Nothing worked to free her.

"Do you have anything to help with her pain?" Ciaran asked Sizx.

She nodded. Madeline felt a needle poke her, and then her head lolled onto Ciaran's shoulder.

CHAPTER 14

Ciaran brought Madeline to the bedchamber where he had previously been resting. He brushed away the tangle of stray brunette curls on her forehead. She was asleep, but the pain still hovered on her face. Dark shadows had formed under her eyes. He rubbed his thumb on the dimple of her left cheek.

Fear clawed at him now. If this pregnancy cost him his wife, he wasn't sure whatever it was he was doing in this universe made any sense.

There was a noise at the door. Ciaran looked up and saw Niw. The old man hesitated for a short moment and asked, "Are you Ciaran LeBlanc?"

It didn't matter whether Niw was Eudaizian or human. There was one thing Ciaran had taken from Earth that he was sure was applicable in any universe—his life experience and his ability to read people. He knew Niw was an honest citizen. Ciaran nodded.

Before Niw could say anything further, Sizx rushed in and had Niw pressed against the wall in a second, her small gun pointed at his neck. "You're not supposed to solicit information, Niw."

"Let him go, Sizx," Ciaran said.

Sizx looked at Ciaran then released Niw. Niw shifted his sore shoulder. "Regarding your wife, I have called my son, Liam. He'll be home shortly and will examine her. He's a medical doctor."

"Thank you. I appreciate it," Ciaran said.

They heard the door open and close. "That must be Liam."

Sizx kept her hand hovered above her gun as a tall man in his mid-thirties with sandy hair and blue eyes entered the room.

"This is Liam," Niw said.

Apparently, Niw had briefed Liam, and the doctor's measured eyes landed directly on Madeline.

"Is she injured?" Liam asked Ciaran.

Ciaran shook his head. "Madeline has to be in Tower One by tomorrow for her officiation of Sciphil One position. I trust you know how important that is to Eudaiz. I sedated her because her pain was bad. I wouldn't care to give her another dose of sedative. Do you have any ideas?"

Madeline stirred in her sleep and awoke. As soon as she opened her eyes, a searing pain shot through her body. Ciaran could read the pain in her eyes as he held her hands. "If you tell me you want the pain to stop, I'll take care of it," Ciaran said.

"How can you say that to me? What do you mean you'll 'take care of it'? These are your children as well," Madeline said.

"If carrying them is going to cost you your life, I'm not going to just sit here and let it happen."

"I'll never forgive you if you do anything to harm our babies, Ciaran."

"I can handle your anger. I'd rather have you live to torment me."

"I can give her something for the pain. We can decide the next step later," Liam said.

"Please," Ciaran said.

The doctor pulled out a compact medical box. He prepared something on a handheld device, and it produced a small, square patch. "Right arm, please," he directed.

Ciaran held Madeline's right arm out, and Liam pressed the patch to the inside of her wrist. It stuck on and then evaporated and absorbed into her skin, providing instant pain relief.

"Thanks, Liam," Ciaran said.

Liam nodded and stepped back respectfully. "She can use this pain suppressor only once every forty days. Each time, it will last only two days."

Madeline sat up. "Thank you," she said.

"What is the safest way to go to Tower One, Sizx? Do you think it's safe to contact Sciphil Seven to get some assistance?" Ciaran asked.

"No, it's not safe. I told Madeline that. Someone at a high level doesn't want you to live until your coronation. If we use the system to contact other Sciphils, it will alert everyone."

"Can we use a private communication channel? I trust Sciphil Two, Ayana, and Sciphil Nine, Pete."

"I don't have a direct private connection, but you do. It should be programmed into your wrist unit. Where is it?" Sizx asked.

"Lost it in the fight," Ciaran mumbled. "But you made the transport arrangement using the system. Wouldn't they know already?"

"No. I made the arrangement for my personal use, telling them my private capsule broke down. They don't know I'm with you and Madeline. But, of course, the council had been alerted about the attack on your capsule, and they know that you're missing."

"Regarding the reserved energy patch, is there a way that I can get around dropping like a stone when the energy runs out?"

Sizx smiled and shook her head. "Not that I know of."

"How do I get a patch like yours? I can't borrow yours all the time."

"You shouldn't abuse it. For ordinary people like me, each person is allowed one patch. It's rechargeable and can be purchased with credit. Most people don't need it. But I don't know about a Sciphil's energy. That information is confidential."

Gaia ran into the room and climbed onto Madeline's bed. "You get well. No more tears," Gaia said and put her arms around Madeline.

"She learned those English words in the last hour?" Madeline asked Niw.

He nodded and smiled. "She has a talent for language."

Madeline played with Gaia's beautiful blond hair. "This is Ciaran," she told Gaia. "He's my husband." And to Ciaran, she said, "And this is Gaia. She gave me flowers in the meadow and called for people to help you."

"Thank you, Gaia. It's a pleasure to meet you." Ciaran smiled.

"You speak like Bran. Are you a prince?" Gaia asked.

Niw interrupted, "She watched all of Bran's recorded holocast."

Madeline smiled, recalling the TV-like screen that she saw in the living room. Holocasts here must be like TV network broadcasts. And the recording must be like video tape. She smiled to herself. This wasn't too bad. She didn't have to ask Ciaran for an explanation every time she ran into a new vocabulary word.

"I'm not a prince, but I can take you to a castle if you like," Ciaran replied to Gaia's question.

Gaia turned around, looking at Niw for permission.

"Yes, you can go if you behave yourself. Now go watch the holocast again and learn some more English," Niw said.

Gaia nodded, jumped off the bed, and ran out of the room.

"Kyle." Madeline was barely audible.

"What?" Ciaran asked, grabbing his daggers.

"It wasn't exactly Kyle, but something really close to him," Madeline elaborated.

"The Black Rock creature," Sizx said, understanding.

"We'll leave right now," Ciaran said and pulled at Madeline. He looked at Niw and Liam. "Anyone else in the family who stays here besides you two and Gaia?"

"No. Only the three of us in this residence," Niw said.

"Get Gaia. All three of you should leave with us," Ciaran said.

Liam rushed to the living room, grabbing Gaia. Niw led the way. "Back door, please," Niw said. They turned down a small corridor and exited the residence.

CHAPTER 15

Niw led the group, running from the alley to the meadow. Carrying Gaia, Liam moved smoothly alongside his father. Ciaran, Madeline, and Sizx followed the Eudaizians. They reached the meadow safely.

"At which gate did you leave the capsule?" Niw asked.

"One," Sizx said.

"We'll cross the meadow then," Liam said.

They followed the alley. In the distance, they could see the shapes of half a dozen men approaching.

"That's them. They have a sense similar to Kyle's," Madeline said.

"Are you sure?" Niw asked. The six men looked like ordinary citizens.

"Black Rock creatures can take any form. You should know that, Niw," Sizx said.

"You all stay here. I'll check them out. I assume the Black Rock creatures don't have blood. Am I correct?" Ciaran asked.

"Yes, but you can't go out there by yourself—there are six of them," Sizx said.

"Easy enough for me to handle if I don't have to worry about three civilians, a pregnant wife, and a child."

"You might as well call me an invalid," Madeline said. "Look, warrior, you won't be able to tell if they're Black Rock creatures or not. I have to get closer to them to confirm it for you. I don't think stabbing people to see if they bleed is a very good idea."

"There's another way to check," Niw said. "Their voices. I've heard they have hollow voices. Let me speak to them." Niw marched toward the group of men.

"Don't let Gaia watch this," Ciaran said to Liam. He grabbed Madeline's hand. "Stay behind me," Ciaran said to her, and Madeline nodded. They walked out from their hiding place. Sizx followed.

Niw approached the group and said something in Eudaizian. They simply stared at Niw.

Ciaran and Madeline approached. "Close enough, Madeline? Can you confirm?"

"Yes. They are Black Rock creatures," Madeline said.

Ciaran charged toward the group of men. He grabbed Niw and spun him toward where Madeline and Sizx stood. He pulled his daggers out, and before the six men could process and react, Ciaran had swung and slashed at them. The creatures' body parts flew through the air. Black liquid gushed from their open wounds and ran onto the ground. Their bodies quickly evaporated.

Sizx and Niw stood shocked, jaws agape. Madeline smiled—she had seen this before. She knew what her warrior husband was capable of. From their hiding place, Liam still covered Gaia's eyes, but he was amazed by the scene that had unfolded before him.

Ciaran holstered his daggers and returned to the group. "We have to go now. Is it still okay to head to gate One, Sizx?"

"No. I've redirected the capsule to gate Two. It'll take a full unit to go through the town," Sizx said.

"Full unit. That's several slots. Meaning several hours in Earth time. We won't make it back to Tower One in time for Madeline's officiation," Ciaran said.

"We have no choice. I'll try to go as fast as possible once we get to the capsule. But to save time, we take the public rail across town," Sizx said as she strode ahead. Everyone followed.

They entered the center of the town. In front of them were endless rows of tall buildings and roads. A sea of people strolled on the street, all beautiful and very friendly. People talked, laughed, made calls on their wrist units. Large public billboards and screens flashed the news in Eudaizian.

If Madeline wasn't mistaken, the news discussed preparations for the coronation.

Several people on the street stopped to hear the news, watching the flashing images of Tower Three where the coronation would be held.

Then an image of Bran during a speech he must have given a long time ago flashed. More people stopped to watch. They cheered when then saw Bran's image. Some had tears in their eyes. As the late king of Eudaiz, Bran seemed to have the respect and love of his people. Bran's speech was in English, and Eudaizian subtitles ran across the bottom of the screen.

"Hurry, it will be your picture up there next." Sizx pulled at Ciaran.

She was right. An image of Ciaran walking out of the tower flashed onto the screen. He looked like a magnificent warrior, a great king. The crowd roared with excitement and joy. Niw, Liam, and Gaia gawked at the screen. Ciaran scurried away from the crowd with Madeline and Sizx.

"Bloody hell," Madeline muttered when she realized Ciaran stuck out like a sore thumb in the sea of Eudaizian civilians. Eudaizians had blonde, blue, or green hair, a milky complexion, and an eye color that matched the hair. None of them had raven black hair like Ciaran. The fact that he was exceptionally tall didn't help his invisibility, either.

Madeline spoke to Sizx, "If you mean we have to get on one of those railed flying capsules over there, how the hell will Ciaran get in without being recognized? I bet they have screens in those, too." Madeline pointed to an array of hanging rails with public capsules traveling efficiently underneath. The capsules stopped at a raised platform where people could get on and off.

Sizx looked at the crowd and said, "We'll take the express. It's quieter. But the computer might ask for verification. I'll see what we can do."

Sizx led the way around a corner. She was right. It was much quieter at the express platform. A capsule the size of a minibus zoomed toward them and stopped as soon as they arrived.

"Very efficient," Madeline commented.

"It operates on sensor distribution," Ciaran said.

They entered the capsule after a group of trendy young people exited. The door closed, and the capsule moved ahead without a sound. There was, indeed, a screen in the capsule that people were watching intently.

Ciaran chose a corner to stand in and faced the wall, pretending to read a notice on the board hanging there.

A man at the far end stopped watching the news. He turned and looked at Gaia. His fair complexion turned dark, and it appeared to have blue current running beneath the skin. His eyes rolled up and turned a glaring red.

Everyone else was busy watching the screen and paid him no attention, but Gaia saw the strange man approaching. She pulled Liam's hand. Liam registered the danger and pushed Gaia behind him.

Ciaran heard Gaia's distress above the noise in the capsule and turned around.

The strange man was a few feet away from Liam. He pulled out something that looked like a handgun. But before he could pull the trigger, Ciaran's dagger lopped off his gun arm. The gun and arm dropped to the floor. Madeline picked up the gun. Wire and cords splayed from the open wound of the broken arm.

"It's a robot," Ciaran muttered.

The other ten civilians in the capsule had noticed the commotion. They swarmed to one end of the capsule to get away from the damaged robot. It pulled out another gun with its other hand.

Ciaran grabbed the gun hand and stabbed at the robot's head, sneaking the skull box open. The robot reached for him with its broken arm. Sizx and Madeline pointed their guns at the robot but didn't have a clear shot. Ciaran stabbed one more time at the motherboard, and the robot stopped moving. He then yanked the board out. The robot dropped to the floor, smoke billowing from its head and eye sockets.

The capsule stopped at the next station. Someone had punched the emergency button, triggering the alarms. People recognized Ciaran. Sirens rang from everywhere in the capsule and the station.

The reek of Kyle filled the air and engulfed Madeline's senses. She peered outside the capsule and saw a small group of creatures charging in their direction from a far corner of the station. Kyle was one of them.

CHAPTER 16

"Kyle is here. Far left corner," Madeline said briskly.

Ciaran scanned the capsule. There was no control panel. "Who's controlling this capsule, Sizx?"

"Central robot," Sizx responded.

"All right. I can't drive it. We've got to get out of here." Ciaran said and dashed quickly out of the capsule. He took his beam-proof vest off and gave it to Liam. "Cover Gaia," he said.

They raced out of the station and ran along a quiet street.

"Now what?" Ciaran asked Sizx.

"They called central. Everyone already knows you're here," Sizx said.

"We'll see Sciphil Seven then. If he's a mole, I'll take care of him. How can we contact him?" Ciaran said.

"Not directly—we'll have to go through the Guard Central. Sciphil Seven would have gotten the alert by now, so he should make himself accessible to you. This way." Sizx pointed toward the far corner. "It will be half a unit on foot."

"That should do. Try to avoid public places. Too many civilians around," Ciaran said.

They moved as fast as they could for another block using back streets. They could see a group of five guards approaching in the distance.

"Are they real guards, Madeline?" Ciaran asked.

"Too far away to tell."

The guards had seen them. Ciaran pushed everyone behind the wall of the station. He walked toward them, with Madeline trailing right behind him. As they got closer, she whispered, "Black Rock creatures."

The creatures pulled guns and shot waves of black laser beams at Ciaran and Madeline. The beams missed and punched deep holes into the walls. Ciaran pushed Madeline behind the wall. With two quick steps, he was on top of it and running toward the creatures from behind.

He leaped from the wall, landing behind them, and pulled out his daggers. Before they had a chance to beam anymore, Ciaran made quick work of them. Soon their body parts lay on the ground, oozing black liquid everywhere before they vanished. Ciaran grabbed the scattered weapons.

Sizx brought Liam, who was holding Gaia in his arms, and Niw out of hiding. They ran toward Ciaran and Madeline.

"We've got to get to the central on a capsule. I don't know who's who on the street anymore," Sizx said.

Ciaran handed Sizx a gun. From behind them, a group of twelve guards appeared.

"Get behind the wall!" Ciaran yelled in warning.

Black beams sprayed the wall just as they ducked behind it. Ciaran rolled out on the ground and shot down three attackers before taking cover back behind the wall.

Madeline spied a blood trail on the ground. "You're shot. Let me see." She turned him around, seeing a gash on his arm.

"Not too bad," Ciaran said and shrugged.

A beam flew from behind them, hitting the wall next to Liam and causing him to stumble and drop Gaia. Ciaran picked the little girl up. "Run," Ciaran said and strode quickly along the wall. Sizx ran along with Liam, and Madeline ran side by side with Niw.

Beams bulleted at them. Madeline and Niw were hit from the back. Madeline had her vest on, but the impact of the beams still dazed her. Ciaran turned and fired at the shooters, taking all four of them down.

Madeline stopped. On the ground, Niw was dead.

"Madeline!" Ciaran called out.

"I'm fine. He's gone."

Madeline saw the sorrow in Liam's eyes. Tears rolled down Gaia's face, but she bit her lips and didn't make a sound.

"Keep going," Ciaran said. Madeline stood and raced alongside him.

"There are five of them left. Can you take two from the ground?" Ciaran asked Madeline.

Having been in similar situations with her husband, Madeline knew it was a rhetorical question, but she answered anyway. "Yes."

Ciaran shoved Gaia to Sizx. "Stay right here," he said then turned around, talking to Madeline. "With me now, Madeline."

They charged toward the other side of the wall. Madeline rolled on the ground, and Ciaran stood tall. Together and at the same time, they sprayed the last five creatures.

Ciaran helped Madeline up. "Are you hit?" Ciaran asked.

Madeline shook her head. "You?"

"No," Ciaran said.

They walked to the other side of the wall. Out of the corner of his eyes, Ciaran saw a creature he'd shot before stand up and point a gun at Madeline.

He pushed Madeline aside, shot the creature, and copped a beam to his chest in return.

Madeline pulled the trigger of her gun. It jammed.

She pulled her sword and charged at the creature. Before she cut its head off, Kyle's voice erupted from its mouth, "I told you, ennead will kill you all."

Madeline roared and swung her sword, detaching the head from the body of the creature.

She scrambled back to Ciaran. He had dropped to the ground, lying in a pool of his own blood.

CHAPTER 17

Madeline sat Ciaran up, leaning him against the wall. He didn't speak. When Ciaran said nothing, she knew it was bad.

"Liam, can you do something?"

Liam looked at the hole the beam had created in Ciaran's chest and said, "We have to go to the medical center, or he'll bleed to death."

The faint sound of a capsule approaching the station echoed in the air. Madeline stood and strode out to the platform so that the sensor got her. The capsule stopped, and the door opened. As soon as it did, she jammed her body against it, holding it open. She pointed the gun into the capsule. "Get out of here. Out now, or I'll shoot."

The Eudaizian passengers didn't understand a word she said, so she swung the gun, gesturing for them to get out of the capsule. They stormed out and ran.

"Get in everyone!" she shouted toward the wall. Liam took Gaia, and Sizx helped Ciaran, and they raced toward the capsule. The door closed behind them. An automatic voice made an announcement in Eudaizian.

Sizx punched the wall of the capsule and cursed in Eudaizian. It was rare to see Sizx lose her composure. She looked at Madeline and Ciaran and translated. "It said we have just committed an act of vandalism, and this capsule will take us straight to jail."

Ciaran sat on the floor, slouched against the wall. He tried to save his strength by not talking. Blood continued to pour from him. Soon there would be nothing left in him. Madeline held her jacket against the wound, applying pressure to stop the blood flow, but nothing seemed to help. Ciaran was as white as a sheet.

"Can they verify us by visual, Sizx?" Ciaran asked.

"No. As far as they know, we could be Black Rock creatures in disguise."

Ciaran was tired. He closed his eyes.

Madeline bit her lip. She couldn't control her tears, but she could control her thinking. There had to be a way out of this. "Is there a control panel in here?" Madeline asked Sizx.

"Data from the rail captured the inside activities—that's why this capsule is sending us to jail. So that means there has to be a control panel and camera in here somewhere."

"Check underneath the alarm button," Ciaran said weakly.

Madeline hurried to the button. There was some kind of screw holding the cover on. She pulled out her dagger and stabbed and scratched at the panel until it opened, revealing a verificator inside. She pressed her palm against it and was verified.

Another announcement. Sizx translated. "It's now sending us to central in District Seven where Sciphil Seven will see us."

"Why the hell do we want to see him now? We've got to get to the medical center!" Madeline exclaimed.

117

Ciaran closed his eyes and said nothing. Madeline knew he was drifting away.

Gaia shrugged out of Ciaran's long vest. She approached Ciaran, tucked away the errant strands of hair covering his face, and wiped the blood smears from his face. Ciaran opened his eyes and looked at her. He smiled at the little girl.

"Don't fall asleep," Gaia said.

"I can't help it, Gaia," Ciaran said. He closed his eyes again.

Gaia reached up and embraced him. A wave of tingling sensation and energy washed over Ciaran. He opened his eyes.

Madeline could see the surge of energy in Ciaran's eyes. She remembered feeling that sensation when Gaia had hugged her at the meadow. Madeline approached the two of them and sat down next to Gaia.

"Gaia, Ciaran is hurt badly. Here." She lifted a layer of Ciaran's jacket, revealing the bleeding wound. "Could you make his pain go away? Make it stop bleeding?" Madeline asked gently.

Ciaran closed his eyes again.

Gaia looked at Madeline, confused. Then the girl looked at Ciaran, who was fading away. Liam and

Sizx realized what Madeline was trying to do and came closer. Gaia looked at Madeline again. "You can do this, Gaia. You can help him," Madeline said.

Gaia placed her hand on Ciaran's wound. She said something in Eudaizian.

"She asks the pain to go away," Sizx translated for them.

Before everyone's astonished eyes, Gaia's hand heated up, and the skin glowed a bright red. Energy sparked somewhere in the capsule, and it jerked a couple of times and then stopped as if its energy had been sucked out. The lights went out, and the engine stopped. The sliding door opened in the middle of the rail, leaving the capsule dangling in the air in between stations.

Gaia looked scared, but she didn't seem to be able to stop the process. So she continued. Underneath her hand, the broken flesh, tissues, skin, and bone regenerated and joined back together. The bleeding stopped, and the wound vanished without leaving a scar.

Ciaran opened his eyes to see Gaia looking at him. She had the smile of an angel, he thought. Then he frowned. On Gaia's left cheek, close to the corner of her eye, a tiny image of a sunflower had appeared. It looked like a glowing tattoo. Gaia saw the change on Ciaran's face, and she rubbed at the sunflower spot.

"Liam," Ciaran called and glanced at Gaia's face. Liam darted over and immediately saw the change to his daughter's face. Gaia withdrew, using her palm to cover the sunflower. Her eyes filled with tears. Ciaran grabbed her hand and gently pulled it from her face.

"Do you know you now have a beautiful flower on your face? Does it hurt?" Ciaran asked.

Gaia shook her head.

"So why are you crying? You're beautiful—even more so with the flower. I've never seen anything like this before." He wiped a tear that had fallen onto Gaia's face. He glanced at Madeline and signaled her to come over.

"Come here, darling. You're beautiful." She took Gaia into her arms, carrying her to a corner and snuggling with her on a bench. Gaia settled into Madeline's chest, sobbed a bit, and fell asleep.

"Do you know what that flower is?" Liam asked Ciaran.

Ciaran shook his head.

"Is it bad?" Liam asked.

"I don't think so. I think it's some kind of mark that represents her ability to transfer energy. I don't know what it is yet, but I'm sure it didn't hurt her," Ciaran said.

Liam nodded. He withdrew to a corner and ruffled his hair in thought.

"Can you think of anything unusual that might have happened to Gaia?" Madeline asked.

Liam shook his head. "We're ordinary Eudaizians, and we've had a very normal life." Liam rested his head in his hands. "I don't know what's happening with her!"

"She said it didn't hurt, and I don't think it's causing her any harm," Sizx said.

"How can you be sure?" Liam exclaimed.

"Shhh!" Madeline asked for silence, but Gaia woke. She turned around, looked at everyone, and smiled. The sunflower on her face had disappeared—she didn't even seem to remember it.

CHAPTER 18

Ciaran, Madeline, Sizx, Liam, and Gaia exited the capsule and walked straight into a long hallway within the District Seven central office. It had taken half a unit to get here, and the time had helped Ciaran gain enough strength to walk by himself. Although Gaia had healed the wound, she could not do anything to replace the blood and energy he had lost.

In the capsule, after the wound healed, Ciaran had verified himself at the control panel in the capsule. It alerted the central robot, recharging the capsule and sending them straight to Sciphil Seven's office.

Ciaran surveyed the long hallway and spotted possible locations of surveillance cameras—and possible escape routes in case things went badly. Gaia looked up at the ceiling and narrowed her eyes at a blinking surveillance camera and a strange-looking light in the area. She pointed her tiny finger at the light and flicked her fingers, giggling when the light went off.

"Gaia," Liam warned her in the dark.

They heard the rumbling sound of someone talking at the other end of the hallway and then footsteps. The light came back on.

A group of three guards walked past. Ciaran quickly glanced at Madeline and got an approving nod, letting him know she sensed no danger from the guards.

A screen flashed on the wall, and text ran across. *"Please approach the verification chamber."*

Ciaran glanced around and saw a screening chamber, similar to the scanner doors used at airports. When Sizx proceeded toward the door, Ciaran said, "Wait. Is this typical when you enter Sciphil offices in civilian districts?"

"Yes," Sizx responded.

A thick American-accented voice came out from the speaker, "Should I escort you up here? Follow the computer prompts please."

"Who are you?" Ciaran asked.

"The person you've come to see," the voice answered.

"How do I know you are who you say you are?" Ciaran asked.

"How do I know you are the people I am supposed to receive?"

"Verify yourself first," Ciaran said.

"You've got to be kidding me!"

Ciaran turned around. "We're leaving."

"All right, all right . . ." A stream of muttered profanity erupted from the speaker. The screen flashed the credentials of Sciphil Seven, Ralph Durant.

"Is this authentic, Sizx?" Ciaran asked.

Sizx nodded.

Ciaran verified his palm prints on a control panel. The green light flashed, and the security door pulled open for the group. Green arrows hovered in the air along the corridor to give them direction.

A short moment later, they entered a round room with multiple screens and control panels.

Sciphil Seven was a tall man with a sturdy face, short brown hair, and honest eyes. It was hard to gauge his age. But time reference seemed to be irrelevant here, Madeline thought. He approached and shook Ciaran's hand, glancing at the whole group.

Ciaran pulled out a chair and sat down without an invitation. He waited for everyone on his side to do the same. Sciphil Seven saw the tension. He strode to the other side of the round table and seated himself.

"Well, given Ayana and Pete made a big deal of this, I'll arrange a capsule and take you back to the Sciphil zone," Ralph said.

"Well, it *is* a big deal. Madeline will go through her officiation and will be Sciphil One soon. Unless you consider your Sciphil position isn't important, I think this is a very big deal," Ciaran said.

Sciphil Seven smirked. "She's your wife."

"I wouldn't take her any other way. She'll soon be my first councillor. I'd imagined we'd be sitting around the same meeting table." Ciaran leaned back in his chair.

Ralph sighed. "Whatever. I'll take you to the Sciphil zone. Consider my pitiful duty done. Like I don't have anything else to do, such as governing a district of more than seventy million citizens. But I won't take civilians to the Sciphil zone." Ralph pointed his chin toward Sizx, Liam, and Gaia.

"It might be against policy, but Liam and Gaia will go to Sciphil Central with us," Ciaran said.

"You're not king until after your coronation. Don't try to order me around."

Sizx's hiss was audible. Sciphil Seven glanced at her and could see that she was clenching her teeth as if wishing she could grind him into dust.

"You're actually quite glamorous when you're not angry, civilian," he said to Sizx.

Ciaran gestured Sizx's silence as he could tell she was about to fly over the table to tackle Sciphil Seven.

"Sizx is not a civilian. If you care for your government, you should know she is the head of the central intelligence, which could not only overtake your district's system but also overwrite everything if she found your system to be inferior and inefficient."

"Her? Head of the intelligence system of Eudaiz? I don't think so," Ralph said.

Sizx sprang to her feet and shrieked, "Who are you to say? *You* are the one who tipped off Ciaran's capsule's position to the Black Rock. You're the mole!"

Ralph stood. "You're the mole, lady. I've been in my office, and I'm verified and have full access. On the contrary, no head of the intelligence system would run around in civilian areas. Plus, you're Eudaizian. Ayana wouldn't appoint natives to take on such important positions."

"She is eighty percent Eudaizian."

Ralph smirked. "It's the twenty percent that counts. Bad news for you, sweetheart. I've just spoken to the central intelligence system. And I'm sure it wasn't you I talked to. Now, do I have to beat the truth out of you, or will you volunteer the information about who hired you?"

Ralph approached Sizx. Ciaran kicked his chair so it skidded out from under the table and stopped right in front of Ralph.

CHAPTER 19

The ground floor of the District Seven civilian office shook with footsteps. Eudaizian soldiers and robotic soldiers rushed toward their bunkers. An officer shouted into the communicator, "Sciphil Seven, please respond, sir! Emergency!"

There was no signal on his machine. He angrily smashed it into the wall and hurried toward the stairs. He pushed the door in, but his body was carried back out, dangling on the claw of a gigantic crab-like creature.

***

Madeline pressed her sword against Ralph's throat. "There is no need for a fight. And there is no need for my husband to move a finger, either. He's your king, and you are to do what you're told. Your district is a huge mess, and still you sit here with noses in the air, accusing people."

"Lady . . ."

"I'm not a lady. I am a Sciphil One-to-be. And as Ciaran's wife, I'd consider myself your Queen-to-be. If you don't have such a position in Eudaiz, let's create one."

"The mole is the blue hair behind you. You're making a big mistake," Ralph said.

"Well, we haven't seen any evidence of her betraying us. On the contrary, she almost died saving us. And while we were out and about in your civilian area, we found concrete evidence of Black Rock spies . . . and chaos," Ciaran said.

"That's total bullshit. Nothing came across in my reports," Ralph snarled.

Ciaran continued, "In those glowing reports of yours, I speculate that there is no information on the number of guards marching around the streets in the name of Eudaizian protection who are actually Black Rock creatures. We killed more than twenty of them on the way here."

"That's a lie."

"The bodies of those Black Rock creatures evaporated and can no longer be found in your system, but Niw Hance's body is still at a rail station behind a side wall. Why don't you go see for yourself?" Ciaran pointed at Liam and Gaia. "He lost his father, and she lost her grandfather. In the blink of an eye, right in the center of the place that you say promises happiness. What do you say to that?"

Ralph stood up. "That's not possible."

Ciaran snatched Ralph and spun him back to where he had been. Gaia tried to subdue her crying, but tears still rolled down her face.

Before Ralph could say anything further, sirens and alarms rang throughout the building.

"What the fuck is that?" Ralph yelped.

"Now you're under attack. Call your head of security," Ciaran said dryly.

Ralph ran to the control panel at the corner of the room, yelling, "Security! Answer me! Security!"

No response.

Ciaran took his beam-proof vest off and shoved it at Liam. "Wrap Gaia up." Then he rushed to the doorway, glanced down the corridor, and closed the door. He checked his guns.

Ralph frantically worked the control panel. "None of my staff are responding."

"They're dead," Sizx mumbled.

"Not possible," Ralph protested.

An explosion echoed up from downstairs, shaking the building.

"How many guards do you have here?" Ciaran asked.

"One hundred and eighty."

"Why don't I hear any movement?"

Ralph pulled at his hair. "Don't tell me they're all gone!"

Ciaran shook his head. "Is this room sealed?"

Ralph nodded.

"Where's your capsule? We have to get out of here."

"Upstairs. But I'm not going anywhere until I sort this out. My guards are heavily armed. I have to check on my people."

"All right, you lead the way. I'll back you," Ciaran said. "Madeline and Sizx, please watch Liam and Gaia. And please stay in this meeting room until we're back."

Ralph pushed the side door open and stormed out into a long corridor. Another explosion came from the far end downstairs, rattling the building again. They scanned the corridor and found no one. Racing through it, they turned a corner into a wide wing that appeared to lead to a capsule station. In front of them, the doors to compartments and chambers had been flung open, and dead guards littered the floor.

Ralph darted toward a body sprawling on the floor, half in and half out of a compartment.

"My head of security," he sighed.

The upper half of the officer's body was covered in holes, steam still escaping the wounds.

"Black beams. I took one this morning. It wasn't pleasant," Ciaran said.

"What's that?" Ralph asked.

"They have the properties of laser beams but are made up largely of dark energy."

Ralph pulled officer's body out of the compartment. "Seriously? My people have been killed, and you're telling me they were shot by magic bullets? How the fuck am I supposed to deal with that?"

"It's not magic. It's dark matter, a relatively unknown substance in the multiverse. You're a Sciphil. Haven't you ever questioned how you can travel between universes or what they're made of?"

"I don't really care." He continued to drag the body. Ciaran pulled him away.

"We have to leave," Ciaran said.

"There are others. Down at the guard center. I have to check on them."

"They didn't respond to your call. They're gone, Ralph," Ciaran said.

Ralph swung toward a wing on their right. Ciaran grabbed him. "Where're you going?"

"Control room. Weapons and access to the capsule terminals are in there. We have to clear it." He shrugged Ciaran's grip off and ran. Ciaran followed him. They found two flying bugs waiting for them in front of the control room.

"Get down." Ciaran flew at Ralph and squashed him down before the two robots sprayed black beams at them. The beams punched holes in the floor, and two of them cut into Ciaran's shoulder.

Ciaran pulled his guns and shot at the flying robots. The guns had no effect. The robots were approaching Ciaran and Ralph again.

"Withdraw. Hurry!" Ciaran said. He stood up and retreated.

CHAPTER 20

At the far end of the corridor, Madeline, Sizx, Liam, and Gaia approached. Madeline could see Ciaran and Ralph running toward them with flying robots at their heels. Madeline pushed the group behind a wall.

Ralph was hit and fell to the ground. Ciaran rolled around the corner. The robots chased him.

Madeline signaled the group to keep quiet. As Ciaran ran by, she jumped out and pulled him into the hiding place.

She stuck her head out to try to calculate the robots' approaching speed. They seemed to have lost Ciaran when he turned the corner. They were scanning the ground and approaching slowly.

"I told you to stay in the meeting room!" Ciaran snarled.

Madeline shrugged. "But I missed you."

Ciaran glared at her.

Sizx pointed her gun at the robot.

"Don't shoot, Sizx! That will lead them straight to us," Ciaran said.

"I'm going to have to ask Gaia to do this," Madeline said to Ciaran.

"Are you sure?" Ciaran asked.

She nodded and turned toward Gaia. "Gaia, Ciaran is hurt. Here, on his shoulder. Could you help him the way you did before?"

Knowing the task now, Gaia nodded.

"Wait and do it when I say so," Madeline said. She looked at the flying robots again, calculating. When they were close enough, she said, "Now, Gaia."

Gaia pressed her small hand on Ciaran's shoulder and did what she had done before. In the process, she sucked the power from her surroundings. The lights in the corridor flickered and went off. The lights on the robots flickered.

Their eyes rolled up and stopped moving. All of the energy in the robots was sucked out, and they shut down completely and dropped to the floor.

Gaia smiled as if she had just finished harvesting flowers in the meadow. No flower image appeared on her face this time.

Ciaran kissed Gaia's forehead. "Thank you," he said. Then he kissed Madeline's cheek. "I'm sorry. I shouldn't have raised my voice at you. You were right to be here. Now we have to get to the control room."

Then he charged out to the corridor toward Ralph. "How badly are you hurt?"

"Got me in the back, but I'm fine. I can move," Ralph moaned and sat up. Ciaran helped him to his feet. Ralph pulled a reserve energy patch from his belt and applied it to his wrist, but it didn't work. He looked at it curiously. "Goddamn it, it's empty." Sizx looked at her wrist unit and cursed. It, too, was dead.

Gaia had drawn the energy from those in her latest stunt.

They heard the rumbling sound of footsteps in the distance. Ciaran charged toward the control room and verified his palm on the control panel. The heavy steel door slid open.

At the far end of the corridor, a group of six creatures approached in the form of guards.

"Here are my guards," Ralph said.

"No, they're Black Rock creatures," Madeline said. "Your guards are dead."

The disguised guards pulled out long guns and started beaming at them.

"Inside. Now!" Ciaran shouted. Madeline grabbed Liam and Gaia, diving into the room. Sizx caught a beam on the leg and fell. Ciaran darted toward her and carried her inside. The door closed. From inside, they could hear the creatures clawing at the door.

"They can't get in here. Don't worry," Ralph said.

Ciaran put Sizx down. "Can you hang on without your reserved energy patch?"

Sizx nodded.

Ciaran had a new gash on his shoulder from a beam he'd taken when he picked Sizx up. Gaia approached to heal it. "No, no, sweetie. Thanks. I can manage this one. Don't heal in here, okay?"

Gaia nodded and sat down in a corner.

"We need the energy," he said to Ralph. "You'll have to put up with your injuries for a little longer.

Can we contact central of Sciphils or make calls from here?" Ralph nodded and got up to man the controls. Ciaran waved him off. "I can do it."

Ciaran turned the communication channel on and looked for Ayana or Pete. The control panel flashed positive signals.

Ayana's voice came across. "What's your status, Ciaran?"

"I've lost my wrist unit and just got a hand on this communication channel now. You know where we are. We're under attack at the moment. Any idea how we can get out of here in one piece?" Ciaran asked.

"You need to get inside Sciphil zone. District One," Ayana said.

"How long will it take to travel from here?" Ciaran asked Ralph.

"The express will take two units. We can be there by the last unit of the night," Ralph said.

"We'll be waiting right at the exit of your capsule when you arrive. Be safe," Ayana said and turned the communicator off.

More banging on the door.

"How do we get to the capsule?" Ciaran asked.

"Side door." Ralph pointed to a steel door located in a corner of the room, and he adjusted his Sciphil sword. He opened a steel cabinet and pulled out two long guns. Ciaran approached, grabbing two guns for himself. Madeline and Sizx did the same with some smaller guns.

Behind them, the main door had been broken down by a robotic arm. Black Rock creatures in guard uniforms stormed in.

"To the side door," Ciaran ordered. Ralph led the group, but Ciaran stayed back, took a stance, and fired at the incoming creatures. They went down like dominos, piling on top of one another. When the flow of robots seemed to stop, Ciaran left the room. He raced to catch up with the group at the far end of the corridor.

Ciaran saw Kyle walk out, appearing from nowhere.

"Down! Right now!" Ciaran yelled.

Everyone dove to the floor immediately. Ciaran rushed forward, unleashing his guns on Kyle. Kyle took a step back and smiled. He wore his beam-proof vest.

On the ground, Ralph raised up and drew his Sciphil sword. "No vest is going to help you with this." He charged at Kyle and slashed.

Kyle pulled a black sword. Ciaran dropped his gun, pulled out his daggers, and moved forward. Ralph gave Kyle a few hard slashes that sliced off his vest. He was much faster and more skilled than Kyle, but the sword Kyle used was superior. With every clash of their swords, Madeline was certain that Ralph would lose.

Ciaran darted in to support Ralph, and Madeline saw the smirk on Kyle's face. It was what he'd been waiting for. If a Sciphil sword couldn't do much damage, what chance did the daggers have? Kyle slashed at Ciaran's arm and kicked him, sending him rolling across the floor. Ralph stabbed at Kyle but missed and received a stab in the back from the black sword. Ciaran charged at Kyle again, fighting without much hope.

Then Madeline remembered something, and things just fell into place. She stood up, pulled out her daggers, and approached Kyle from behind.

"Yo!" she called out.

Kyle slashed at Ciaran then turned to receive two wounds from Madeline's daggers. She didn't have the strength to cause much damage, but one of the daggers carried Gaia's blood from when she'd cut herself and bled on it in the meadow. For an evil soul like Kyle, the blood of an innocent was lethal. It was a speculation on her part, but it worked.

Smoke came from the wound, and Kyle screamed in pain. He slumped to the floor, and it looked as if he'd die like the other Black Rock creatures. But something sparked inside him under his skin. Kyle surged up and charged at Madeline. In anticipation of Kyle's action, Ciaran flew over to cover her, suffering a slash to his back.

Kyle ran away and vanished down the long corridor.

Sizx checked on Ralph, who was lying on the ground, gasping for air. "Can you move? Tell me what you need."

"I've lost my district," Ralph whispered.

"Yes. But you have to survive to take it back," Ciaran said.

Ralph shook his head. "Too late. I'm done. I haven't a successor for Sciphil Seven position. I'm sorry, Ciaran. You'll have to take care of that."

"I'll take you to central. We have a doctor there," Ciaran said.

Ralph shook his head. "Don't waste your time... I ... need ..."

Sizx asked, "Where is your object?"

"... Ring ..." Ralph was almost out of breath.

Sizx pulled the stone ring he was wearing out from his finger, and placed it in her palm. "I'll take it to the chapel for you," Sizx said.

"Thank ... you ..."

"Where's your family? Who should we ..." Madeline asked, but before she could finish her sentence, Ralph drew in his last breath and died. In a short moment, his body glowed and then disintegrated into a beam of light. The light absorbed into the ring on Sizx's palm.

Seeing the questions in Ciaran's and Madeline's eyes, Sizx said, "Your soul will rest in an object of your choice after you die. This is how it works in Eudaiz."

Ciaran nodded and looked away. Madeline knew he was thinking of his father. He didn't know about this, so he wouldn't have any idea where Bran had parked his soul after he died.

The group hurried into the capsule. It zoomed away along the dark tunnel toward the safety zone.

Ciaran looked at the control panel, the map, the journey progress. "It's going fast. We'll get to District One just before the last unit of the night."

"Let me stop your bleeding," Madeline offered and then mused, "The last unit of the night—in time for you to drop like a stone." She came up behind Ciaran.

He turned around, lifted her chin, rubbed his thumb on the dimple of her left cheek, and kissed her. "How are mother and children?"

"Just fine," she said, kissing him back.

Gaia poured out a stream of something in Eudaizian. Liam smiled and shook his head. Sizx rolled her eyes.

"Do we need to know what she said?" Madeline asked.

"Nope." Liam smiled.

One unit and a half went past. Ciaran checked the monitor. "We're nearly there. A few more . . ." He couldn't remember the term.

"Slots," Sizx said and smiled.

Ciaran shook his head to stay alert and leaned against the wall of the capsule. Madeline saw his signs of fatigue but said nothing.

The capsule slowed considerably. Red alarm lights flashed across the control panel, indicating an unexpected energy shortage and expected stoppage of the capsule. Sizx rushed to the computer control panel. "We should be able to get more from the central robot," Sizx said as she pressed buttons and pulled handles. "They're not responding," she muttered.

Ciaran looked at the panel. "We're being cut off. They don't know yet that we have a shortage of energy. We have to keep our momentum. We're nearly there. As long as the capsule doesn't slow down any further, the momentum will get us there." He pointed to the map on the screen.

But the capsule slowed yet again.

"Someone's stopping us," Ciaran said as he observed the energy indicator decreasing rapidly.

CHAPTER 21

Ciaran braced his hands on the wall of the capsule as it slowed significantly in speed. "I can't let us lose momentum. I can't let you miss your officiation, Madeline."

She said nothing but just embraced him. She had done that once during the Daimon Gate tests when she sensed that he was about to experience a life and death battle. With her psychic ability, she could sense danger, but she didn't necessarily know how to handle it.

"What are you going to do?" she asked.

He lifted her chin up and kissed her. A long, deep, and passionate kiss. He finished with her lips and wiped the tear on her face away. "Can you forgive me if I can't help you in the last leg to your tower?"

"You will be with me all the way," she said firmly.

He nodded. "I'm going to push the capsule. I did this before on Earth. I used my energy to send Bran all the way from Earth to Eudaiz. So a little push to this capsule shouldn't be too bad."

She nodded. "If you must," she muttered and looked away.

Ciaran approached Gaia. "Gaia, when you heal my injuries, you must feel as if you're drawing some kind of power and putting it in your hand. Is that right?"

Gaia nodded.

"So here is what I want you to do. Come here." He brought her to the control panel. "This green button is to keep this capsule moving ahead. What I want you to do is to pull the power out of me and push it into that button. Do you understand?"

Gaia frowned.

"Do you understand what I said, Gaia? Don't take the power from anywhere else or the capsule will stop. We have to push it forward, or everyone in here will die. So hold my hand, draw the power from my hand only, and push that green button."

Gaia looked at Ciaran.

"Can you do that?" Ciaran asked.

Gaia looked at Madeline. "Madeline?" she called.

"Yes, Gaia."

"If I do this, will it make you really sad? You look really sad right now."

Madeline came to Gaia. She couldn't stop her tears, but she could try to convince the girl that it was okay for her to help. "I'm sad, Gaia. I can't help it. But you have to do what Ciaran asked. Everyone here needs you to do that."

Gaia nodded. She held Ciaran's hand and did what he instructed.

The capsule jerked, roared, and then zoomed ahead, exceeding its original speed.

Ciaran slumped to the floor. In his mind's eye, he saw millions of black stars and lightning. The energy flowed out of him like a raging river pouring into the ocean. He braced himself against the wall and tried to stay conscious.

Madeline went to him. "Don't touch me," he said. Even speaking that short sentence taxed him. He closed his eyes and focused. Gaia wanted to withdraw her hand, but Ciaran held fast, and she couldn't wiggle free. With her other hand, she continued to push the green button.

They zoomed into the Sciphil central platform. The capsule slowed down and stopped, and Ciaran finally let go of Gaia's hand.

He was drowning.

He saw nothing but darkness. He was falling into a bottomless black hole. There was neither air nor gravity. He hovered and then dropped again. A spark of lightning cut through the darkness. One more. And another. Ciaran realized that it wasn't lightning, but sparks of energy. He saw a blur of light coming from the terminal.

He felt the heat of the energy from Gaia's body and realized she was holding him. The lights in the capsule flickered and went out.

He opened his eyes and felt Madeline's tears raining down on his face. "There now! Welcome back, my warrior," she said, brushing his hair out of his face.

"What happened?" he asked.

"When we arrived, Gaia drew the energy from the capsule and put it back into you."

Ciaran could feel he was lying on the floor of the station. He tried to sit up. "Easy now. You still don't have much energy at all."

"Are we at Tower One?" Ciaran asked.

"Yes. Not at the gate, but we can make our way to it. We've made it, Ciaran."

"Ayana and Pete aren't here?"

She shook her head and helped Ciaran stand.

Sizx approached. "I've never been here before. But I think it's a bit quiet to be the Tower One secured zone. If there are no people guards, there at least have to be some robotic guards."

"I'm afraid the lady is right," Kyle spoke from a corner.

CHAPTER 22

Madeline and Sizx drew their guns, aiming at Kyle.

Kyle laughed. "Let me give you a tip, ladies. The only weapon that will kill me is the king Sciphil sword, which none of you has. Now, I'm going to be a gentleman here. I'll take your king-to-be with me and let the ladies live. I'd love to kill him, but at the moment, he's worth more to me alive than dead. How does that sound?"

"I need your reserved energy patch, Sizx," Ciaran said between his teeth.

"It was ruined at District Seven," Sizx said.

Knowing Kyle couldn't handle the dagger with Gaia's blood stain, Madeline drew it and charged at Kyle. He blocked the dagger and staggered back. Then she saw a strange look in his eyes as if he was trying something new.

She knew Kyle was a mind-bender. In their previous encounters on Earth, she'd seen him control people's minds and make them do whatever he pleased, including killing themselves. His ability didn't work on Madeline and Ciaran, and apparently it didn't work on Eudaizians like Sizx, either.

Madeline felt a slight prick at the back of her neck, and then something resembling a smile crossed Kyle's face.

"You're with child. Wait. *Children*," he smirked. "I can see three minds in you. Hello. Welcome to Eudaiz, children."

She felt a pang in her stomach. Kyle was peeling the painkiller away and was waking the children. He couldn't control *her* mind, but he could certainly work on the babies.

Sizx lunged at Kyle and copped a kick, flying backward toward the far end of the station and crashing into a wall. *Where is Ciaran?* Madeline thought as she retained her stance, trying to suppress the pain that had started to hit her in waves. She couldn't afford to turn around to look for Ciaran and leave Kyle unattended.

Kyle advanced. Madeline didn't withdraw but gripped her dagger harder and charged. Kyle grabbed her dagger hand, twisted the dagger from it, and tossed her several feet away. From the ground, she could see Ciaran standing with Gaia and Liam next to him.

"I believe you just hurt my wife. I can't accept that," Ciaran growled.

Kyle laughed. "I don't believe you're in a position to say that—"

Before Kyle could finish his sentence, Ciaran reached his hand out. Gaia grabbed it.

The capsule burst into flame, and an explosion echoed through the station, numbing the mind and plunging the entire place into darkness. Under the light of the fire, Ciaran aimed the gun at Kyle.

"Ready, Gaia. Fire," Ciaran said.

The beam coming out from the gun was like a tidal wave of energy. Kyle was instantly swept away. From whatever dimension he was thrown into, his voice echoed back, "Ennead will kill you all . . ."

Darkness.

One light flickered. Then the next. And the next. The station lights were back on. Ciaran darted toward Madeline and asked, "Are you okay?"

"I wish you'd told me you could draw energy, put it back into you, recover, and shoot Kyle away like that. Would have saved me a lot of worries," she grumbled.

"It wasn't me—it was Gaia. And I had no idea it would work," Ciaran said patiently.

"I'm sorry. I know. I don't mean to be petulant." She clutched at her stomach again.

The pain was bad. There was hardly a physical sign of pregnancy at all. But she could feel every blow of her children kicking inside her. Ciaran could see how bad her pain was. "Is there anything you can give her to ease the pain?" Ciaran asked Liam.

He shook his head.

"I can handle it," Madeline said.

From a corner, Sizx had finished reconnecting the communications panel. "This is not the station to Tower One. Somebody manipulated the central system and sent us here."

"Where are we then? Can we make it to the tower in time?" Madeline asked.

"If you're in pain, we are going to a medical center, not the tower," Ciaran growled.

"If I don't take the position in time, Eudaiz is doomed. There's no point in going to a medical center. They'll find us and kill us, Ciaran."

"If you're alive, we can always figure things out."

"Get out of here," Sizx shouted and raced out of the station. As soon as they made it outside, a spark flashed behind them, and the station became a volcano of metal and flames.

Ayana and Pete arrived in two private capsules. They jumped out of their vehicles.

"Wrong station. We were waiting at Tower One. Get in or you'll be late!" Ayana waved frantically. Madeline and Ciaran got into her capsule. Liam, Gaia, and Sizx climbed into Pete's. The two capsules flew away.

CHAPTER 23

The area leading to Tower One was flooded with crab-like creatures and ugly zombies.

Ciaran said, "This explains why Kyle was at the station by himself. He wasn't receiving the best support from whoever hired him. These creatures are the most primitive soldiers I've ever seen. Can you handle them yourself?"

Ayana smiled. "I could have killed them before, but that would have alerted whoever was using them. I want them to think we're in trouble so they don't pay too much attention to you."

"You're a mastermind, Ayana," Ciaran said.

"I learned from the best," Ayana said. A flash of sorrow crossed her face. Leaning against the capsule wall, Madeline saw the look and knew that it was caused by the pain of Bran's death. This woman had loved Bran deeply.

"Madeline is pregnant, and she's in a lot of pain. Is there anything she can do to help it subside?" Ciaran asked.

Ayana looked at Madeline. "How long have you been pregnant?"

"I'm within the first stage of gestation. I know the process, Ayana. But I have to get through this officiation first. There's no time to do anything else," Madeline said.

Ayana nodded. "In theory, when you receive your Sciphil One eudqi, it will ease your pain. You'll be very strong. As for how long it will last and whether you'll still have to follow the traditional way of giving birth, I don't know."

Ciaran nodded. "That's good enough for now."

Ayana hovered the capsule at the gate of the Tower, dropped Madeline and Ciaran off, and returned to savage the army of ugly Black Rock creatures.

***

Up close, Tower One was a mountain of cement and steel—a gigantic, round structure that reached to the sky. Ciaran approached the control panel and pressed his left palm to it. The structure grumbled, and the heavy walls shifted, revealing the entrance. Ciaran held Madeline's hand, and they raced into Tower One, the shadow of the imposing tower swallowing them.

The grand round dome opened before their eyes, inviting them inside.

He led her to the cleansing chamber and waited as she walked through it.

When she stepped out, her Sciphil clothes had been fitted tightly to her body. The material looked soft and comfortable, but it served as protection from all beams and most weapons. She wore her hair loose, a sea of brunette waves wrapping around her shoulders. Her face was radiant.

Ciaran looked at Madeline with love and admiration. His beautiful wife remained unchanged on the outside, but on the inside, she was ready to take on this new responsibility. She was born to be his first councillor, his warrior.

She stepped into the tall glass chamber while Ciaran manned the control panel and activated the machine. The glass door sealed.

Then she stumbled. He could see in her expression that the pain had worsened. She braced her hands on the glass door and drew in deep breaths.

He yanked and kicked at the door, but it wouldn't open for him. "Can you get out?" he asked.

She pulled the door and shook her head.

He could see Madeline almost passing out with the pain. He darted to the control panel. His fingers flew over the keyboard. Regardless of the codes and commands he entered, the door wouldn't budge. The round lid on top of the glass chamber started to spin. The process had started. There was no way to reverse it.

Ciaran ran back to the glass chamber where he stood hopelessly. There was no way he could help his wife.

She crouched on the floor now, breathing heavily.

She looked up at him with tears in her eyes.

Ciaran had never felt so helpless in his life. He wanted to destroy the chamber to save his wife.

He could. He was capable. But what would be the point? She would be killed in the process.

A cone of light brushed her back, traveling from the ceiling to the chamber.

"Please hang on, Madeline. I love you. You have to survive this. Absorb the power of the energy. You'll be fine."

Tears rolled down her face. She didn't look as if she could hang on. He traced his hand along the glass wall. She tried to put her hand on his. But she couldn't even reach up.

Then she looked at him. In front of him, a miracle occurred.

She gently put her hand on her tummy. "Children, listen to your mother. Whatever it is that you're doing is hurting me. If you are my good children, please stay still. Stop hurting me. Mommy loves you. If you keep doing this, you're going to kill me."

One moment passed. And another. Then she stood up and looked at him through the glass wall. She smiled.

It dawned on him then. They didn't have ordinary children. Their children had been conceived in the Red Stage of the Daimon Gate tests. They were designated to be the best beings in the cosmos. Of course they were smart.

He felt delirious seeing Madeline finally pain-free.

The top of the glass chamber opened to a funnel which connected the box to an endless astronomical space. Thousands of light beams poured down through the funnel to shower Madeline. The room sparkled in brilliant white and blue light.

From inside the glass box, Madeline looked at Ciaran and smiled. She glowed like an angel. Ciaran knew the eudqi was flowing into her body and mind.

As the energy flow stopped, the funnel shrank and shriveled into a cone-shaped blue and white stone the size of a fist, fixed on top of the box. The glass box stopped spinning.

The screen inside the glass chamber flashed a message. "*A major source of energy was corrupted. Alternate energy was used. Please activate the ennead code to accept the energy.*"

"Ciaran! What does that mean?" Madeline called out, her voice shaking.

She didn't need to elaborate—he knew what it was. Kyle had been plotting this. Her precognition had indicated it. He cursed himself now that he hadn't paid it enough attention.

With a calm voice, Ciaran said, "You have received the eudqi of Sciphil One. But you have to accept the alternative source of energy. These energy sources work in harmony and as a combined source of power. If you don't accept, the whole pack of energy will be withdrawn. That will kill you and our children."

He roared with anger inside and hoped Madeline couldn't read his mind at the moment.

Whoever it was who wanted him dead had corrupted one source of energy, forcing the Eudaizian system to replace it with an alternative source. This move was much too smart for Kyle. Even if Kyle was a part of the game, Ciaran didn't believe he could pull this stunt together himself without any help.

Kyle's biggest contribution to this scheme would be that he knew their weakness—or more precisely, Ciaran's weakness—emotion. Emotional attachment to humankind. The sort of emotion that would cloud his judgment.

If a wrong choice was made, the officiation process wouldn't be completed—and Madeline would die. His children would be gone as well.

Ciaran's knees weakened.

But there was no time or room for fear. He paced around the glass chamber like a wolf while Madeline held her breath, waiting.

Ennead code . . . what could that be?

Ciaran thought. He speculated. And he decided to gamble. "Madeline, do you trust me?" he asked.

"Yes." She looked at him as she said so to let him see her confidence in him.

"Then type in Atum."

She did. The computer screen flashed green light. *"Level one confirmed."*

Before he had a chance to feel better, the computer presented them with nine options. "To complete the process, please suggest which dimension you would collapse."

Ciaran was furious. Someone was playing on their weaknesses. They had gotten the first part right. Ennead, in this case, was a group of nine deities in Egyptian mythology created by the god Atum. But Ciaran knew his knowledge of Egyptian mythology was limited.

The nine options presented were coded with the names of nine Egyptian pyramids. It wasn't the pyramid they had to choose but rather an astrological dimension associated with it. Collapsing a dimension meant killing all creatures living in it. It could be Earth, other planets, the Daimon Gate where his parents lived, or maybe even Eudaiz.

There wasn't enough time for him to do research, to decide which was which.

Madeline looked at him. "Ciaran, do you trust me?"

He stared at his wife and realized just then how formidable she was. "Yes, of course."

She smiled at him. Then she turned around and placed her palm on the control panel. Her hand glowed. She closed her eyes and pressed a button.

The air around her exploded with particles of light. The screen flashed and showed the text, *"The officiation process has been completed. Congratulations and welcome Sciphil One, Madeline LeBlanc."*

CHAPTER 24

Later, Madeline was on the floor next to the glass chamber, and Ciaran was on top of her. He kissed her, long and deep. She groaned as his hands moved slowly over her body. There was nothing more to explore. He knew her body well. But still, he was doing it so slowly that it was torturous—the excruciating pain of pleasure.

"How did you know that Atum was the first code?" she asked.

"Speculation. Plus years of experience studying criminal and corrupted minds to design computer games." He kept himself busy with her body. "How did you know which option to choose?" he asked.

"A hunch," she said.

He purred audibly.

Maybe he thought it was cool that she had made a decision that carried the lives of millions on merely a hunch? No. She didn't think so. She knew he probably supposed she had used her psychic ability to read the mind of the individual who had corrupted the system and placed the code.

Even though that person might be hundreds of dimensions away.

Even though he might reside in hell.

The connection he had put into the first level of the test had given her a gateway to track his mind.

Having received the full power of her Sciphil One energy, she wasn't just a psychic now, she was a mind tracker, and she could hear his evil mind calling out the option that he wished she wouldn't choose. So she selected that very option.

"The next thing is your coronation, isn't that right?" Madeline asked, playing with Ciaran's hair.

"We can worry about that tomorrow."

"We've lost Sciphil Seven. How are we going to replace him?"

"We have the whole council. We're not on our own," he grumbled as she was distracting him from the most important thing at the moment—exploring her body.

"Yeah, some of that very council want you dead. If Sciphil One position is this hard already, how difficult will it be when it comes to your coronation?"

"We're coming in expecting more enemies than friends. This is a new world for us. We're making changes, and nobody likes changes."

"What's the first thing you'd change when you become king?"

"The design of their capsules. They're not my taste."

Madeline chuckled, remembering Ciaran's passion for sports cars in London.

"This is the officiation of Sciphil One. Shouldn't it be some sort of big deal in Eudaiz?" she asked, groaning again at his touch.

"I'm sure it is. There are nine Sciphils who govern the entire universe of more than six hundred billion civilians. I'm sure this is a huge event." He continued to assault her with kisses and gentle caresses while she grabbed at the glass panel, trying to maintain her composure.

"Where are my clothes? I kinda liked them. You didn't rip them, did you?" She was breathing heavily. His movements were so strong it used up a lot of her energy.

"The clothes suit you. But you look best without them on," he said.

"Are you sure we aren't being broadcast everywhere given this is a big event?" she gasped as she exploded with pleasure when he plunged into the heat of her.

He was so focused he didn't even hear her question.

On all the streets of Eudaiz, in all the districts, on public screens and private screens the breaking news of the latest and significant event of their universe was being broadcast live.

The eyes of hundreds of millions of civilians were glued to the screens.

The crowds roared in celebration of the new and very different Sciphil One.

In a control center of the central intelligence, Sizx was smiling as she watched a monitor with split screens. On one screen, the raw footage of what was happening in Tower One was playing. On the other, the screen marked 'cleared for public broadcast', was the edited version of the breaking news to the Eudaizian public.

PART TWO

KNIGHT & PAWN

CHAPTER 25

The soft, muddy black substance coated his flesh and mixed with his blood as he sank deeper into the ground. Black Rock—the universe of darkness—was swallowing him alive for his betrayal of trust.

He hadn't thought it would end this way. Kyle Wolf. He had once been the only Eudaizian in the Sciphil council. How was it possible he could climb so high and fail so miserably?

Eudaiz was a universe of true happiness, where virtuous people lived in harmony. One upon a time, he thought he understood what it took to be happy. He had been born a Eudaizian. His talent had been recognized by the council, and he was offered a Sciphil position.

Sciphil—Scientist Philosopher—was a term they had brought from Earth in a language they called English. Kyle snorted to himself and spat out some blood. The council of nine humans had arrived in Eudaiz hundreds of years ago and built the sovereignty that now governed more than six hundred billion Eudaizian citizens.

Then they had taken in one Eudaizian to the council. *Him.* So why had it been such a big deal when he asked for more privileges? He was the only native person on the council. He ought to be important.

He wanted happiness. Just like everyone else.

"Chiara," he whispered to himself. "What did you want that I didn't have?"

Kyle tried, but he couldn't lift himself up from the mud. It glued him down, sucking every drop of strength out of him.

During the last fight with Ciaran LeBlanc, Ciaran had shot him with something powered by an incredible force. Ordinary weapons couldn't cause him much damage. So he hadn't expected Ciaran's gun to do any, either.

Apparently, he was wrong.

He got hit, flew out of Eudaiz's dimension, and dropped into some kind of black hole. He'd done his best to crawl back to Black Rock. But here, in his temporary home, even the ground was eating him alive.

A blast of freezing air brushed at his body from the behind. This wasn't the Black Rock air. This was the presence of his master.

The master stepped out from behind Kyle and looked down at him. Before this man, Kyle had never thought a human could walk the land of Black Rock.

"Master, I've done everything I could. Please give me another chance. I'll capture Ciaran for you."

The voice that came out of the man was like music. His English was similar to Ciaran's. Certainly not at all like Madeline's New York accent. But it didn't matter where his Master was from. Kyle worried only about whether he was angry enough to kill him.

"Why should I give you another chance? The list of your failures could wrap around the Earth three times. It's not as if I gave you complicated tasks to do. Only greed would make a smart man like you fail those simple assignments."

"No, Master. I did what you wanted me to."

"Really? I wanted you to find out where Ciaran and Madeline were. Instead, you tried to capture them yourself and almost killed them. I asked you to capture Sciphil Seven. You killed the man. I asked you to tip Madeline off about the ennead to see how Ciaran solved the problem. You tried to capture them *again* and got blown up. And now you're lying here like a piece of garbage."

"I'm sorry. I thought you wanted them captured."

"I have my plans, and it's not for you to know them. I haven't much invested in you. I should have ended your pathetic life. Perhaps I should just cut my losses now."

"No, no. Please, Master. I have some news you could use."

"Don't try my patience. You have one last chance. Speak."

"Madeline is pregnant."

The Master smirked. "Well now. That *is* good news. Do you know what kind of kid it is?"

Kyle frowned. "What do you mean? I know she's having twins."

"Are they children conceived at the Red Stage of the Daimon Gate?"

"I don't know, Master."

"All right. The news is good enough. You've finally done something right. And now you have two new tasks. And if you complete them successfully, I'll reconsider my initial offer to you. First, capture the children for me. Alive. I can't emphasize the *alive* part strongly enough. Second, because you killed Sciphil Seven, they'll have to fill that position with someone else right away. Wait until after he or she takes over the position and capture the person as well. Again, *alive*."

"Yes, Master."

"I have a plan that your pathetic mind wouldn't be able to grasp. So do only what you are told, and then I'll give the Sciphil Four position back to you. Ciaran LeBlanc is mine to kill. If you ever again attempt to jeopardize my plans, I'll bury you with whomever you kill. Understood?"

"Yes, Master," he whimpered the answer as his master reached his hand out to pull him up from the mud of death.

CHAPTER 26

Madeline sat at the bedside and watched her husband sleeping peacefully. She could never get bored by the sight of him. God had been very unfair to all other humans when he had created Ciaran, giving him the best of everything.

She was only thirty-three, and time had taken a toll on her. Her brunette locks had gotten thinner and had stopped behaving well, especially first thing in the morning. She found a goddamn wrinkle at the corner of her left eye yesterday. And she swore her hips had gained one whole unforgivable inch overnight.

On the contrary, Ciaran was four years older than she. He handled a global conglomerate on Earth. He had fought his way through life and death battles to get to this universe, and in the process, he had been injured—should she dare use the word *died?*—multiple times. Yet he looked the same. He hadn't aged a bit.

Sinfully handsome with long, raven-black hair that almost touched his shoulders. Intense gray eyes and a God-given face that made her stomach churn nonstop with lust. And the long, lean line of his toned muscles was beyond description.

He stirred and opened his eyes.

She climbed onto the bed. "Hey there! Good morning! How many fingers?" She held up three fingers in front of his face.

"Three."

"And who am I?"

"Madeline LeBlanc, my beautiful wife, Sciphil One, and my first councillor."

"How many wives do you have?"

"Three, excluding you." Ciaran laughed. "I don't have a concussion, Madeline. Stop fussing." He pulled her into his arms and rubbed his thumb across the dimple on her left cheek. "I'm good as new. And before you roll your beautiful eyes, tell me how the mother and babies are doing?"

"The whole gang is fine," she said as she curled into him. She loved the way their bodies fit together, like two perfectly matching pieces of a jigsaw puzzle. "I didn't like the sound of your head hitting the floor last night," she told him. "We ought to do something about it."

"We talked about this, Madeline. Until after my coronation, I have to run on temporary energy. What I could do to reduce my odds of hitting hard objects is to lie down before the energy runs out. I know it's not a perfect solution. But my energy isn't a priority right now. You and the children are."

She clutched her tummy absently and curled deeper into his arms. "I was wondering if I could go back to Earth and deliver the twins there. You know, do it the traditional way. Your mother did that. And look how you turned out." She smiled at him and gave him a loving, doe-eyed look.

He kissed her forehead. "But my mother left Eudaiz immediately after she knew she was pregnant. She didn't accept any Sciphil energy, medicine, or treatment in this universe for the pregnancy. You, on the other hand, have received all of that. I think it's too risky to deliver the children on Earth now."

She said nothing. She knew he was right. She sighed.

"On the bright side, I don't have to go through the big-belly period," she mumbled, making Ciaran laugh.

The gestation period in Eudaiz was twenty-eight days. Within the first seven days, the baby was taken out of the mother's body and placed in a birth chamber.

She had been told many times that the technology in this universe had worked for hundreds of years without fail. Still, it was a scary thought for someone who had just left Earth like her.

The door security patch flashed a green light once, and the door slid open. The home robot, human in size and shape, entered. Ciaran sat up in bed.

"One green light isn't equivalent to a knock, and we haven't answered the door yet, Robert," Ciaran said.

"How many flashing lights would you like me to adjust to, Ciaran?" the robot asked.

Ciaran shook his head. "You will storm into our bedroom regardless. What's the matter?"

"Sciphil Two, Ayana Dee, left a message for you in the control room."

Ciaran nodded. "All right. I'll see to it as soon as I can."

Robert approached the bed and flashed a scanning light beam up and down Ciaran's body. "Your body mass index is perfect for six foot three and thirty-seven years of Earth biological age. Disease free. Physical strength, sixty percent. Artificial energy, ninety percent. Natural energy, zero percent."

Ciaran arched an eyebrow. "I didn't ask for a scan. But thank you."

Robert said, "This is a routine scan. Your biological age is locked in at thirty-seven. It is necessary to benchmark for future improvements and adjustments."

"You're saying I'll remain at this biological age forever?"

"No. When Bran LeBlanc, the previous king, officiated your role, he had locked you in at your prime age. Future adjustments will have to be made to maintain this status."

"What about Madeline? Can you examine her now?" Ciaran asked.

Madeline sat deeper into the bed. "Skip the body index part. I just want to know if the children are healthy."

The robot scanned her and said, "Madeline's biological age was supposed to be locked in during Sciphil One officiation. However, the process could not be done because she is pregnant."

Madeline rolled her eyes. "Breaking news! Are the children healthy, though?"

"I do not have available data to benchmark children's profiles. This can be done at medical centers. However, there is a warning of which I need to inform you."

Madeline's heart skipped a beat, and she saw Ciaran's eyes darken.

Robert continued, "Nine Sciphils hold the nine crucial pillars of power in Eudaiz. Our universe is one of the most prosperous and powerful in the multiverse. We always have adversaries wanting to take our resources. In addition to attacking the Sciphils, there is a fifty percent chance they will attack the weak links."

Ciaran narrowed his eyes. "You mean our attachments and dependents."

"Affirmative. Friends, relatives, and family members of Sciphils have a fifty percent chance of being attacked outside Eudaiz. Seventy percent inside Eudaiz. Eighty percent if they are children and infants. You are the king Sciphil, Ciaran. The probability that your children will be attacked at birth is ninety-nine point ninety-nine percent."

CHAPTER 27

Madeline strode alongside Ciaran, following the long grand hallway which connected to the reception room of Sciphil Three residence. She wished the hallway was longer, but unfortunately, the walk had come to an end. They had arrived at the reception room, finding Jennifer, Ciaran's mother, waiting.

Madeline tried her best not to squirm.

Jennifer was formidable and literally glowed with energy, power, and graciousness. Her striking blue eyes with their unusual almond shapes made her perfectly oval face seem sharper. Those eyes could slice Madeline in half just with a quick glance. Although she was sure Jennifer never intended to intimidate her, her stomach still always did a somersault in front of her mother-in-law.

"You look well, Mother. How's Father?" Ciaran asked.

"We're fine. How are the four of you?"

Madeline couldn't see her own face, but she knew it was bright red. She swore she could feel the four-day-old babies kicking inside her.

"We're all well," Ciaran said.

Madeline rubbed her tummy absently.

Jennifer arched an eyebrow. "Really? I heard you were attacked in District Seven. Sciphil Seven died, and you barely made it to your Sciphil One officiation."

Ciaran narrowed his eyes. "That's Eudaiz's internal information, Mother."

"Oh, don't pull that look on me, Ciaran. I didn't use any technology to spy on your universe. Although I could have. Tadgh told me about this," Jennifer said.

Ciaran shook his head. "I thought he was busy with his training. He must have told you already that he is to replace the late Sciphil Seven. And his officiation will take place the day after tomorrow. It's a significant event. I'm sure you know that."

Tadgh was Ciaran's younger brother and one of the nicest people Madeline had ever met. Madeline knew Ciaran loved his brother although he never admitted to it. Tadgh had gone through the Daimon Gate tests with them and had completed his tests successfully.

"Well, yes, he is busy. But that didn't stop him from giving his mother a call. He's a good boy," Jennifer said and smiled at Ciaran. Madeline did a mental eye roll. Both of them were mama's boys. Jennifer loved her sons terribly.

Madeline wondered if she could ever do to her twins what Jennifer did for Ciaran and Tadgh. Only time would tell.

"I'm here because of your pregnancy, Madeline."

She almost jumped out of her skin but gained her composure quickly and said, "The home robot has predicted that it's likely the babies will be attacked."

Jennifer nodded. "This will be the best chance ever to attack Eudaiz. The millions of your enemies will try to get your children. You might or might not be able to negotiate with them. You might be righteous enough not to give in, protecting Eudaiz at the cost of your own family. But you are both humans. This will weaken you, whichever way it goes. And that is what your adversaries are waiting for."

"And you know all this because?" Ciaran asked.

Jennifer turned and looked at him. "Because I am your mother."

Ciaran stared, expecting a continuation.

Then she smiled. "And because I was once trained as a Sciphil. I was once married to the king Sciphil, whether I liked it or not. And because I am now married to the most virtuous man in the cosmos, I've seen every face of politics in this multiverse. Thus, I did not need a computer to tell me that they would go after your children."

Ciaran said, "I wager you've come here with a solution as well. You couldn't use the communication channel because the conversation would be recorded. And you know we have a mole in our executives, so if the information leaked, we're in trouble."

Jennifer smiled. "I don't have a total solution, but I can suggest something. Have you met Sciphil Six, Janei Chatel?"

Ciaran shook his head.

Jennifer said, "I was her successor. When she knew about my pregnancy, she helped me. I owe her my life—and yours—for that, Ciaran. We are going to go to her for help. It has to be done face to face. And you have to somehow delete the record of our visit to Sciphil Six. I don't want to put her in danger."

"You said you don't have a total solution. What's the next option if this doesn't work?" Ciaran asked.

"Janei is more than a hundred years old. She has plenty of experience. She will have a suggestion for an alternative solution."

Ciaran nodded. Then he moved to a computer control panel to make a call. A short moment later, Sizx breezed into the room.

"This is Sizx, the Eudaizian head of intelligence. This is my mother, Jennifer," Ciaran introduced. Sizx and Jennifer gave each other courtesy nods.

"How did you get here so fast?" Madeline asked.

"I came because of this." She opened her palm and revealed a reserved energy patch. Then, before Madeline's astonished eyes, she approached Ciaran and grabbed his wrist to take a look at his unit. "Ninety percent is good. But keep this just in case you have an eventful day." She slid the patch into Ciaran's pocket.

"I was just about to arrange that," Madeline lied.

She knew Ciaran relied heavily on artificial energy and had borrowed the patch from Sizx several times before. It was like spare batteries. She could have arranged that. But one thing had led to another, and they'd had a very busy couple of days. She'd forgotten.

"Thank you, Sizx. I'll return it to you. I'd like to borrow your frequency detector," Ciaran said.

"All right." Sizx peeled the device off her belt and handed it to Ciaran. "Is there anything else I can do for you?"

"This will be all for now. Thank you," Ciaran responded.

"I'll return to central then." Sizx raised up on her tiptoes and kissed Ciaran's cheek. "Be safe," she said. Then she nodded a goodbye to everyone, turned on her heel, swinging her magnificent blue hair, and sashayed her perfect body out of the room.

Ciaran must have seen the look on Madeline's face. He cleared his throat and said, "I'll use this as a jammer to delete records of our movement. Let's go, shall we?" He approached the side door and pointed the device, working on jamming the signals.

Jennifer walked past Madeline toward the door. She whispered, "You've got competition, Madeline. But don't worry, I'm on your side."

Madeline clutched slightly at her tummy. She thought she had just felt a pang—or maybe it was just her imagination.

CHAPTER 28

Ciaran, Madeline, and Jennifer rushed toward the private capsule platform. It was like having a private subway system in the backyard. The tunnel was sealed and had no other access point except for the door from their private residence. The capsule—the main means of transportation in Eudaiz—looked like a gigantic bullet and was the size of a small train compartment.

On the way, Ciaran pointed the machine at surveillance cameras and anything that resembled an electronic device. They entered the capsule, and he worked on the machine a little more, then he closed the door and activated the capsule.

He keyed in District Six Sciphil residence and entered the address. The capsule shuddered as it woke up and then zoomed along the dark tunnel.

On the wall was a map showing the journey's progress. It was quiet inside the capsule. There was no engine noise. Nothing except the clock ticking.

Wait. Eudaiz didn't use the same time reference as Earth. There was nothing even remotely similar to a clock in here. It suddenly dawned on Madeline that she was imagining the ticking internally. The pain of the pregnancy had returned. It was pounding, hammering on her nerves like a bomb countdown.

Madeline let out the breath she'd been holding and sat down. Ciaran crouched next to her. He squeezed her hands. "You have to tell me when the pain comes back."

Madeline nodded and looked away.

The pain was pounding again.

"I have a deal to make with you regarding our children," she said.

Ciaran arched an eyebrow. "I hope you didn't promise them to anyone?"

Madeline spoke briskly as the pain started to swirl in her head. "I want to name our son, and you get to name our daughter."

"You can name both, Madeline. I don't mind."

Madeline breathed heavily. She grabbed her stomach, but she kept her eyes fixed on Ciaran, trying to maintain a neutral expression. "The son. Just him. What's the name of the god whose toe I broke at Mon Ciel?"

"Coeus. And he's not a god. He's a Titan who represented the inquisitive mind in Greek mythology. And you didn't break a god's toe. You broke the toe of a statute. What's up, Madeline?"

A trickle of sweat ran down her temple. She spoke so fast she stuttered. "I-I . . . at Mon Ciel, when Stefan killed Mrs. Rutherford, I promised the god . . . th-the Titan . . . th-that if you were safe from Stefan, I would name our son after him. I keep my promises. What about Caedmon? It means wise warrior in Gaelic."

"Yes, Madeline. It's fine." Ciaran looked at her. More sweat ran down her forehead and face.

"Caedmon it is, right?" She let out a breath and bent down, putting her head between her knees.

"Madeline, look at me. What's going on? Are you in pain again? Tell me, please."

"No, I'm fine," she tried to assure him.

Ciaran tried to make her look at him, but she would not. He turned and looked at Jennifer.

"She's in pain," Jennifer confirmed.

"Madeline." Ciaran gently lifted her face up and saw the sweat and tears rolling down her face. He sat on the bench and reached over to pull her into his arms, rocking her. "We're nearly there. We'll find a way out of this."

Madeline snuggled into Ciaran's chest. "It'll pass. The pain will settle in a bit," she said.

When the capsule signaled the trip was complete, and the door slid open, Ciaran sprang to his feet, carrying Madeline. She shifted in his arms.

"Put me down, Ciaran. I can walk."

"Where to, Mother?" Ciaran asked Jennifer.

"Please," Madeline insisted. Ciaran put her down and slid his arm around her waist to hold her body against his. Jennifer led the way to a dimly lit stone arch.

In a haze of pain and confusion, Madeline was still able to sense the different vibe of the place. *What a contrast*, she thought. The old stone looked odd against the shiny metal of the capsule platform. It wouldn't surprise her if torches lit the corridor instead of lights. Her intuition proved correct. The long corridor was illuminated by wall torches. It was like walking out of a metro station from the future right into a medieval chamber.

A stone panel swung open as they approached. Ciaran glanced around, locating and marking escape routes and electronic equipment. They entered a grand hall with stone sculptures and magnificent artwork. A glorious fireplace warmed the room, casting a flickering light on the figure of a tall woman standing with her back to them. She turned.

Janei Chatel, more than a hundred years old, looked more like a Greek goddess in her thirties and was radiant in a long red dress that swept to the floor. *Anyone who looks like this at a hundred years of age has to be a vampire,* Madeline thought.

"Jennifer! Long time no see. You look beautiful, as usual," Janei's voice sang with a mild accent.

The voice of surreality, Madeline thought.

"It's been as long as Ciaran's life since we've seen each other. I see you're well. I told Ciaran he owes you his life."

Janei cast Ciaran and Madeline a warm and affectionate glance. "There's no need for such formality. He is now my king, and Madeline is the first Sciphil. I'd say we're colleagues. Is that the right term in modern language, Ciaran?"

"I apologize for being abrupt. We haven't much time," Ciaran spoke.

"I know your situation. And I know of a solution. But it can't be done in Eudaiz."

"I can't go back to Earth now." Madeline tried to suppress her pain.

"If it's not Earth that you mean, where then?" Ciaran asked.

A smirk crossed Janei's face. "Saving Jennifer and you wasn't a waste after all. Indeed, I wasn't referring to Earth. But before I give you the solution, I have a small favor to ask."

Ciaran, Madeline, and Jennifer stared. Madeline felt Ciaran's hand tighten on hers.

"I don't do anything for nothing. I didn't ask Jennifer for anything because she had nothing to give, but I know one day you will be standing in front of me in power. Am I right?" Janei smiled. "It wasn't my time then to demand. But it is now."

Ciaran's eyes darkened. "What do you want?"

"You're having twins. A boy and a girl. I want your daughter as my successor."

"How dare you!" Ciaran snarled.

Then before Madeline and Jennifer could react, he instantly calmed down. "I agree."

His icy voice bounced off the stone walls and cut into Madeline's heart. But she knew him. She knew his logic. Madeline glanced at Jennifer and saw her standing immobile with an expressionless face.

Mother and son, what a perfect pair, Madeline thought.

"Madeline, do you agree?" Ciaran asked.

"Yes." She swallowed her tears and trusted Ciaran's instincts.

Janei nodded and turned on her heel. The three of them followed. There was no sign of anyone on the premises. They walked through a long, arched corridor of stone which led to a dungeon. Janei pushed at a heavy oak door. It squeaked open, and torches inside flickered.

The room was round with a fifty-foot-tall ceiling. The air was so shallow that it made Ciaran, Madeline, and Jennifer dizzy. Ciaran wrapped his arm around Madeline's shoulders as she swayed.

"In the middle of the room is a dimensional gateway. Walk through that, and you will meet someone who has the solution to your problem."

"How can we be sure this isn't a gateway to oblivion? Bran was lost in one of those for thirty-three years," Ciaran asked.

"You don't have many choices, Ciaran. That gateway. Earth. Or the medical chamber in Eudaiz."

From behind Ciaran, Jennifer pushed her way through to the middle of the room.

"Mother!" Ciaran shouted as Jennifer disappeared. He pulled his dagger and pressed it to Janei's throat. She staggered back against the wall. But the expression on her face did not waver. Her sharp eyes locked on Ciaran's in challenge.

"Jennifer will be back, Ciaran. I can feel her nearby," Madeline said.

Ciaran withdrew his dagger, and Jennifer reappeared in the middle of the room, walking toward them.

"The gateway is fine," Jennifer said.

"Mother, you can't act like Tadgh," Ciaran raised his voice at her.

"You should say he acts like *me*. He's my son. So are you. My sons do not stand around, pondering indefinitely, when we have a situation at hand. Are you coming or not?"

Ciaran grumbled something in French that didn't sound very amiable. Madeline grabbed his hand and moved toward the middle of the room.

As soon as they crossed the midpoint of the room, they stepped into the pitch-black weightlessness of a dimensional gateway.

***

In the dark hole Kyle called his temporary workspace, a human-shaped creature as pale as a vampire stood shaking, waiting for instructions.

"Place six spies at the medical center in District Six and twelve at the outskirts of Sciphil Six residence. If they exit Sciphil Six residence with the children, take them right there. If not, wait until they go to the medical center and grab the babies at the birth chamber."

After the creature had scurried away, Kyle turned on an audio communication channel and said in Eudaizian, "Great information on District Six. Thank you. I will compensate you well for that. Listen, before we move on to the next step, there's a blue-haired chick at the intelligence center. She constantly interferes with our communication. Get rid of her."

CHAPTER 29

This other dimension didn't feel any different from Eudaiz, Madeline mused. They walked onto a quiet street in a charming but ancient town.

"Home," Jennifer whispered.

Ciaran was surprised. None of the houses lining the street looked like Mon Ciel, their mansion in Henley-on-Thames, England. He glanced again at the landscape in front of them and recognized it as Jennifer's hometown in Ireland.

"The Irish countryside in another universe," Ciaran muttered. He wished he could find out whether the village, the houses along the road, and the people going about their everyday business were simulated or real. But there was no time to explore now.

Jennifer rushed toward a small alley. Ciaran and Madeline followed. They exited the alley and entered a secluded meadow full of wild roses. Madeline remembered them from the Daimon Gate and District Seven.

At the edge of the flowery meadow, there was a country house, imposing in its size and aura. Jennifer scurried to the house, her footsteps as light as a woman in her twenties. Ciaran took Madeline's hand to keep up with his mother.

As soon as they reached the front gate, the door swung open. The aroma of wildflowers and something baking greeted them. The familiar earthy scent brought tears to Madeline's eyes.

Ciaran pulled her into his arms and kissed her temple, "After this, I'll take you back to New York and buy you a bakery that makes only your favorite bagels. How does that sound?"

She nodded and smiled.

A robotic voice spoke up. "Please come inside."

"I wouldn't be as surprised if I'd heard a cow speak," she muttered.

Ciaran merely smiled. The tranquility of this place was too suspicious for his liking.

They crossed a large living area with a twenty-two-seat wooden table located in the middle. Without instruction or invitation, Jennifer walked directly to a small wing and strode down the corridor. She inhaled the wonderful scent in the air, traced her fingers along the dark wooden rail as she walked, and turned down another hall.

At the far end of the hall stood a tall woman with flaming red hair. She turned around.

"Moira," Jennifer spoke the name as if she doubted her eyes. She didn't even realize she was speaking aloud.

Moira smiled. Except for the hair color, the woman and Jennifer had similar features—oval faces, milky complexions, deep blue eyes—very striking and mysterious. Moira looked to be in her late fifties, sixties at most. *Maybe that's my mother's cousin*, Ciaran thought, mentally searching his family tree.

"Welcome to iilos—not with a capital letter, it is. We are not a proper dimension. And iilos is not a proper place," Moira said. Ireland's brogue sang in her voice like an old soothing lullaby. "It's nice to see you in person, Jennifer."

There were tears in Jennifer's eyes. They rolled down her cheeks. It was a long moment before she could compose herself enough to face Ciaran and Madeline.

"This is Moira Wyse, my great ancestor who lived in the 1500s. I've lost count of the generations in between us. She was the first in our family to marry into the LeBlancs—Pierre LeBlanc's wife. This is"—

"I know who they are," Moira cut in. She walked toward Ciaran and Madeline. Her gait was smooth as if she floated rather than walked.

Ciaran pushed Madeline slightly behind him.

Moira grinned. "Well, well! How protective you are of your woman. That's the most valuable trait of the LeBlanc men, is it not, Jennifer?"

"Indeed."

"You ought to bring your younger one here to visit me. Tadgh, isn't that his name?"

"It is."

"What's iilos?" Ciaran asked.

Moira smiled. "Tenacious curiosity. A common trait in the LeBlanc line. Iilos is a place that hovers in a special dimension in time and space."

Ciaran remembered the file he'd read in the control room at his residence—the history of Eudaiz. He remembered the names of the first Sciphils. He said, "Pierre LeBlanc was the first Sciphil Three, the first king of Eudaiz. You married him. What was your role in the council? I understand—and can tolerate—the concept of dimensional time. But if you are truly from the 1500s, that's a stretch even for me to accept. Why did your husband die, and how are you still alive after all these years?"

"You have to be more open than that, Ciaran. You are in a place of impossibilities." Moira smiled.

Ciaran shook his head, realizing Moira was cleverly avoiding his question. But he had a more urgent matter at hand than prying into her background. "At the moment, one thing is of the utmost importance to us." He wrapped his arm around Madeline's shoulders. "Janei said you'd have a solution."

Moira nodded. "Indeed, I do. But first you have to understand the curved time concept. This is an outer layer of Eudaiz. I control both the time and space of the entry and the exit."

Ciaran nodded. "I know the concept. You continue to expand this dimension outward, and that's how you remain exactly as you were five hundred years ago. Madeline could have the children here. We could leave Eudaiz with her pregnant and arrive back at the same time, the children having been born safely. But do you have the technology to do it?"

Moira cast a warm glance at Jennifer. "Your son's worth every drop of your sweat and tears, isn't he?" Moira said.

Jennifer stiffened and replied harshly, "My son is who he is because of his upbringing. It had nothing to do with where or how he was born."

"When Janei told me about your pregnancy with Ciaran, I instructed her on how to help you, Jennifer. I don't approve of what Bran did to you. You may call it rape, but the conception of Ciaran during the Red Stage of the Daimon Gate was the ultimate achievement of your life. Children conceived there are the best in the cosmos. And now we are about to have two more." Moira gestured toward Madeline.

Tears filled Jennifer's eyes. "I don't need the best. I just want my children and grandchildren."

"We are not commodities, Moira. And if you think you're going to keep my children—for whatever reason—you're mistaken." Ciaran again pushed Madeline behind him. She grabbed her midsection as the pain intensified.

"I have a vested interest in your children. If not for them, what do I get for helping you?"

"Nobody takes our children," Madeline said. She shrugged herself out of Ciaran's supporting arms. Leaning against a wall, she slid down to the floor. Beads of sweat and tears covered her face. Her breathing was shallow, and her eyes bloodshot.

Ciaran pulled her into his arms and rocked her. He held her tightly while her body shivered from the pain. He shot a frantic look at Jennifer, begging for support.

"You are our ancestor. You ought to help them," Jennifer told Moira.

"Because I am your ancestor, the children will be safer with me than in a birth chamber in Eudaiz."

Ciaran asked, "If you want our children because they were conceived at the Red Stage of the Daimon Gate test, why didn't you want *me* when you found out my mother was pregnant?"

"That was more than thirty years ago. I didn't have the technology I needed."

"You want our children for *experiments?* For *testing?* There's no way I'm going to let you do that!" Madeline cried.

Ciaran jumped to his feet, pulled out his dagger, and pointed it at Moira.

"You're smart enough not to kill me because doing so won't help your wife. Don't wait until you have to decide between mother and children. She doesn't look like she can hang on that long," Moira deadpanned.

Ciaran turned around and found that Madeline had passed out in Jennifer's arms.

CHAPTER 30

In District Nine of Eudaiz, Tadgh scurried out of the training chamber. His head was pounding with a headache, and his muscles vibrated with pain from the boredom of sitting still. The days he'd traveled extravagantly on Earth, vegged out in the tropical forests of Asia, and ridden wild animals in Africa were long gone. He was only three years younger than Ciaran, but his maturity was about ten years less. And he was okay with that.

He had been letting Ciaran take care of the family business and had gotten away with it for years. Ciaran preferred it that way because it meant he could concentrate on the family business rather than cleaning up Tadgh's messes.

What had gotten him here to Eudaiz was the only time Tadgh had been seriously involved in the family's business. He loved his family and his brother. But this training was seriously boring him to tears. He didn't even want to think about the serious administrative duty that would come with the Sciphil Seven position after he had taken it.

Will I have to sit in an office? Tadgh wondered, shaking his head and shuddering at the thought.

Tadgh looked around and was pleased that the venue was quiet. He turned on the communication function of his wrist unit and called his girlfriend, Jo. He hadn't seen her for days, and that was torturous.

Then from the corner of his eye, Tadgh saw a tiny, yellow, puppy-like creature. It made him think of TJ, their Alaskan malamute in England. He hoped the staff they had put in place had taken good care of their puppy.

Tadgh crouched and reached his hand out. "Hey!"

The creature looked at him, blinked its eyes. Then he remembered what Sciphil Nine had said in the Sciphil residential area—only Sciphils and authorized officers were allowed. No creatures or civilians.

So why was there a dog here? Tadgh jerked his hand back, but it was too late for him. The creature grew in a flash into a gigantic, spider-shaped space creature and charged at him. And all he had in his hand at that point was the wrist unit that he was going to use as a cell phone.

***

In iilos, all Madeline wanted was to hear Ciaran's voice and to feel his hands grasping hers. Her body seemed to be full of knives and needles. With every movement she made, the sharp edges cut into her veins, her flesh, and her mind. It felt as if someone were using a chain saw to separate her body parts, shoving steel hands inside her to rearrange her organs.

And then she heard Ciaran's voice. He was saying something about long-lasting moments, about cherishing the time they had together. He was making promises to her, promises of things she couldn't hear. She felt the grip of his hands. She tried to grab them back, but her fingers wouldn't obey. She felt the warmth of his body, the gentleness of his lips on her forehead and her cheek.

And then she dropped out from the light and the sound again.

She opened her eyes, and they met the deep-colored wooden ceiling. The ceiling swung and whirled for a short moment and then steadied. After the organ shuffling she had just been through, Madeline felt she might finally be back to her solid form. From past experience of the times she had been in the care of Ciaran, she knew that as soon as she stirred, he would leap to her bedside, elegant as always. She needed to see him, so Madeline stirred.

But instead of leaping to the bed this time, Ciaran staggered.

"How are you feeling?" he asked, tracing his fingers along her jawline and brushing the dimple on her left cheek. Except for his beautiful and intense gray eyes, which were unwavering and focused on her, Ciaran's face looked as if he had just battled several planets in the galaxy. She didn't need to ask to see his energy patch to know it was approaching the level of nonexistence.

She felt a tingle on her right wrist, and energy flowed into her body from a patch. In no time, she felt almost back to normal. "How are the children?" Madeline asked.

"They're fine. You can't see them just yet. But I've seen their vitals. They're perfect, Mother." Ciaran smiled and smoothened her hair.

Madeline sat up.

"Are you okay to get up?"

"I'm very sure I can push you over with my little finger right now. What did you have to promise Moira to get her help?"

"Not much . . ."

Madeline raised an eyebrow. She didn't believe him, but instead of arguing, she needed to take action. Madeline got up off the bed. Her energy was fully charged thanks to the patch. She felt like superwoman. She grabbed her jacket, her vest, her weapons, and put her gear on as efficiently as a soldier. "We have to get you and the children out of here. I'll take care of that. I'm a hell of a fighter."

"I beg your pardon?" Ciaran blinked and shook his head as the energy drained out of him with every word he spoke.

"You've used all of your energy, and you're wearing the energy patch Sizx gave you. I bet that was low, too. We can't leave here without the children. I think when I was out of it, you probably figured out how to bring the children to safety—and worked out a deal to get Moira's cooperation."

Ciaran nodded. He stood leaning against the wall, looking at Madeline. The corner of his lips quirked.

"What did you promise her? And please don't say 'not much.' Last time you said that you almost died in the Daimon Gate fulfilling your promises."

A hint of a smile crossed Ciaran's face as he said, "Not much."

Madeline approached him, swinging gentle punches at his chest. He grabbed her hands, spun her around, backed her into the wall, and kissed her. The kiss was deep, rough, and possessive. She understood what he had gone through when she was out. That was an area over which his authority and power had no control. Regardless of how well he could negotiate with or bully his opponents, when it came to Madeline having to pull her own weight to survive, he felt his powerlessness.

When he finished kissing her, his full body weight collapsed, pressing on her. She lowered him onto a chair.

"What did you promise?" She snatched his wrist and took a look. "Jesus Christ! Six percent, Ciaran.

You can't keep doing this!" She yanked at his hand to haul him up from his seat. Ciaran leaned his head into her shoulder, on the verge of passing out.

He whispered into her ear. "I bluff. I promised her something I couldn't do. But because of that, she won't let me die. She will give me some energy. And she will pry for information. Don't let her mess with my head. Push right to the edge. Leave her no time and no other options but to give me the energy and take nothing from me . . ."

That was all he could say. His entire body weight collapsed onto Madeline. As much as she tried to hold onto him, he dropped to the floor like a stone.

"Moira!" Madeline shouted.

CHAPTER 31

In District Six, Sizx pressed her palm to the security panel of her small apartment. The green light flashed, and she pushed the door in. Her place was small but comfortable in a common zone in the civilian area of District Six.

As the head of intelligence of Eudaiz, she was entitled to a larger and more secure residence in an exclusive zone. Everyone was equal in Eudaiz. It wasn't a privilege that the council granted her. It was for her own safety.

Her high position in the government made her a possible target for adversaries. Innocent civilians in Eudaiz could live in the peaceful environment, well-protected by the council of Sciphils. But the higher the person's position on the government ladder, the less naive he could be.

She'd heard that Earth, where the Sciphils came from, was a hard place to live. That humans' minds, bodies, and spirits were trained for battle. That was why native Eudaizians never moved up too far into the government zone. Eudaizians were too naive to participate in politics, her boss had told her before she decided to take on this career path. But she had talent, and she wanted to contribute.

From the corner of her eye, Sizx saw a couple of shadows in her garden. She put on her personal laser beam and sneaked quietly along the corridor toward the side door. She could see them now, and she was sure they were Black Rock creatures.

They didn't bother with disguises. The civilians of District Six had never had a sighting of Black Rock spies.

She switched on the communicator in her wrist unit.

She could call the guards.

But then she looked again.

There were only a couple of them, and they obviously didn't think they needed more than that to handle a woman.

Sizx smiled. She was no ordinary woman. She turned the communicator off.

***

In iilos, after Madeline called out for help, the door of the chamber slid open immediately as if Moira had been standing right there—waiting, spying. Madeline knew now why Ciaran had whispered his instructions into her ear. Not that she knew what to do with them. She had to talk to him about this—he assumed too much of her.

Moira whirled in, followed by four men who efficiently placed Ciaran on the exact bed Madeline had lain on before. They opened a panel on the wall, revealing a series of buttons.

A curved glass lid came down onto the bed, sealing it. The main light was turned off in the room, leaving only the illumination of the dim light from the control panels and the top of the glass lid. Madeline could see a part of the floor shifting. The room was detaching itself, moving.

Moira stepped into the area near the bed. Madeline jumped onto it, too, just as a wall closed behind her and the room turned into a capsule. She couldn't tell they had moved, but she was sure they had.

The wall door slid open to reveal a gigantic area that looked like a factory. They pushed the bed into a horizontal cylinder. The glass lid had been removed by a robotic arm. Moira stayed outside, controlling a panel of monitors and buttons. Inside the cylinder, the men attached shiny silver patches to both of Ciaran's wrists.

They attached two to his chest and were about to attach two more to his temples when Madeline stormed into the cylinder. "Stop! Remove the ones on his chest."

The men stopped in confusion. They looked to Moira, who arched an eyebrow at Madeline.

"We need to check his vital signs. He has only two percent left. We have to hurry," Moira said.

"Out!" Madeline shouted at the technicians in the cylinder. They stared at her but didn't move.

"Get out of there," Moira directed.

They left the cylinder without question.

Madeline peeled the patches off Ciaran's chest. "As far as I know, energy comes in via the wrists. That's the only place I'll allow you to attach any kind of connection to his body."

"You know nothing about technology, Madeline. You're risking his life right now."

"He will only take energy from you. When he's up and aware, he'll decide what else he needs. That's all I need to know."

"I won't inject energy if I can't monitor his vital signs. He hasn't much left. He'll die—and that will be your fault."

"He's far too important to your project for you to let him die. Inject the energy and nothing else." Madeline positioned herself next to Ciaran's bed and stared straight at Moira. Her demeanor was as dark and aggressive as that of a wolf. Moira shifted and nodded at her soldiers.

"Remove her," Moira said.

The soldiers approached the cylinder. Madeline drew her dagger and pressed it against Ciaran's neck. "Let me help you, Moira. You want him dead?"

"You wouldn't," Moira growled.

Madeline pressed the blade of the dagger harder, setting loose a stream of blood.

"At the time we decided to enter the Daimon Gate, we realized that every moment we survived together was a bonus. He would rather die than let you manipulate his mind. If this is the end of us, then so be it."

Moira stared at Madeline, and Madeline stared back. They acknowledged the fact that they shared the most profound of emotions—a love for their men.

The monitor next to Moira beeped. She glanced at it and saw the one percent signal. "Get out!" she shouted at Madeline.

Madeline dove out of the cylinder and rolled on the floor. The door of the cylinder slammed shut behind her. Moira darted toward the control panel, slamming her palm on the command button. The steel inner layer of the cylinder spun, counting every percent of energy charged. Madeline hunched over the monitor. It felt like decades.

Ninety percent.

Ninety-five percent.

Ninety-nine percent.

One hundred percent.

The cylinder stopped spinning. The door swung open. Madeline stormed inside.

CHAPTER 32

Sizx snapped her reserved energy patch onto a docking station in her small bedroom to recharge. The fight with the creatures had consumed some of her energy. She wanted to make sure she had enough for the day. Today was the officiation day of Sciphil Seven. As head of central intelligence, she had to be sure nothing went wrong.

Perhaps she shouldn't have fought the creatures and should have called the guards instead. But since when did she do what she was supposed to do.

Ciaran's arrival had sparked life into her work. Into maybe more than just work. She had a feeling her life had started to get a whole lot more complicated. But she didn't have time to think about that at the moment.

She engaged the communication channel. "Report to me after the network is connected. You have exactly two units and ninety-eight slots to get this done."

Sizx smiled to herself, imagining Ciaran would wince hearing the time reference in Eudaiz.

"Let's see," she muttered as she typed into her computer. "That would equal ten hours and fifty-three minutes in Earth time, Ciaran. Your brother will become Sciphil Seven in such a short time. You should be pleased," she said to herself.

***

In iilos, Madeline was watching Ciaran snap his weapons into place. "I'm sorry about the cut," Madeline said. Her voice shook a bit.

"What cut?" Ciaran asked.

She gestured to his neck. He touched it and found the bleeding wound where she had pressed the dagger. He looked at her and then pulled her into his arms. "I'm sorry. I'll never ask you to do that again."

Madeline knew her husband understood how hard it was for her to gamble with his life. She wasn't built for it, and it had taken a toll on her emotionally. But his understanding was all she needed now. And understanding was what they had plenty of in their relationship.

They entered a wooden cabin. In one corner, Jennifer sat on a chair, reading on a portable device. When Moira turned her back to Jennifer, Madeline caught Ciaran and his mother exchanging looks. Jennifer nodded slightly. Madeline couldn't make sense of their exchange, but she stayed close to Ciaran as she knew something was likely to happen.

Madeline knew that behind the wooden façade of the cabin was metal, and anything inside the room could possibly be flipped out as a control panel. She was sure there were spy cameras everywhere. She knew Ciaran had thoroughly scanned the environment and planned the escape routes in his head, but he couldn't communicate the plan without being heard.

Moira pressed her palm to the wooden wall. A rectangular section became a glass panel and revealed a room beyond the wall. In the middle of this room stood two large steel boxes as tall as a mainframe computer.

Madeline and Ciaran looked through the glass window—in the boxes were their children. She could see that even Ciaran was shocked. In contrast to what they had expected, there were no babies in tubes, floating in liquid, and connected to cords and wires. There were simply two boxes standing in the middle of the room.

"The boy is in the box on the left," explained Moira. "He came first. They're both healthy. At the moment, they're merely substance and matter. In a few days, you will begin to see shapes. At that point, a panel on the box will become transparent so that we can do visual inspections. The room is now sealed and completely self-sufficient. The material that comprises the box will generate energy and supply the babies with what they need," Moira lectured as if delivering a scientific report.

Ciaran inhaled and glanced briefly at Jennifer. Madeline felt his hand clench slightly. "Is this technology similar to that in Eudaiz?" Ciaran asked Moira.

"This is much more than technology. But the short answer is no. It is not the same."

"By self-sufficient, do you mean the chamber could operate anywhere on its own, even in another dimension? If this place is attacked, can we move the chamber elsewhere?" Ciaran asked.

"You don't have to worry. The chance of attack does not exist here." Moira sounded annoyed.

"You said this place is a place of impossibilities. And anything can happen here."

Moira arched an eyebrow. "What do you want, Ciaran?"

"My wife, my kids, and my mother stay within the Daimon Gate, under the protection of the Host and the gate council." Ciaran gazed at Moira sternly.

Madeline understood Ciaran's plan. Daimon Gate would be a brilliant place to keep the children. It was independent of the multiverse and would be the ultimate protection for the children. The Host was Conan, Ciaran's father. She could not ask for more security than that.

Moira's eyes darkened. "Do you think I'm stupid?" She raised a hand to straighten the throw on her shoulders, and as quick as lightning, Ciaran yanked it off. It tore a part of her dress, leaving Moira's shoulder and arm bare. She staggered back, hissing. "How dare you!"

Ciaran darted forward and yanked her wristband off.

He stepped back. "I apologize, Moira. I can't let you call your soldiers. We have to get out of here, and you're going with us. Otherwise, they'll shoot at the capsule."

Jennifer scurried to the control panel as Ciaran covered Moira's mouth so she couldn't scream.

"I jammed all the cameras as you asked. The device from the blue-haired girl has been quite useful. The training I received from Bran years ago doesn't seem to be a waste, does it?" Jennifer said.

"Thank you, Mother," Ciaran said, willing himself not to think too much about what his mother had just said. Bran's name coming out of his mother's mouth was salt in a raw wound.

The cabin closed up and transformed itself into mobile, detached capsule. Moira struggled in Ciaran's arms. The floor shifted a bit but then returned to its initial state. Jennifer cursed.

"The third button on the left, Mother. You have to dial manually. Then the second handle at the bottom. You have to steer it." Ciaran gave the instructions while still hanging on to Moira, who kicked, mumbled, and struggled to break free.

Madeline walked toward Moira. She swung her arm and gave her a hard smack. Moira's eyes rolled up, and her head lolled onto Ciaran's shoulder. Ciaran smiled and shook his head. He put Moira down on a chair and left Madeline to handle the woman then dashed toward the control panel to prepare for their escape.

The cabin totally detached from the platform and zoomed away.

Once they were out in the dark and outer sphere, Ciaran said, "The navigator isn't working."

CHAPTER 33

"**A**re you sure they aren't growing the children up in there, too?" Kyle shouted into a communicator. "How could it possibly take that long? Send a spy inside. I can't spare twelve men just to gawk at the place."

He slammed the channel shut and picked up another one. "What? I don't want to hear bad news. Don't tell me you can't handle a woman." He grabbed his sword and slashed at the table, cutting it in half. "You useless sons of bitches!" he shouted into his communicator.

***

The capsule traveled in between universes. At the beginning, it was hard to navigate because iilos was not a proper dimension. And because the navigator didn't work, Madeline had to use her psychic mind tracker to find general direction and guide Ciaran.

When they got closer to the Daimon Gate, Jennifer could give them precise directions and open the gate for them.

Suddenly, they heard a thud. The capsule landed violently, tilting to one side. Ciaran rushed toward the glass window to view the baby chamber, letting out a sigh of relief upon seeing the two boxes still intact.

The sudden impact jolted Moira. She awoke and sprang to her feet, panting and disoriented.

"We're inside the Daimon Gate. I apologize for my roughness before. You're free to go, but the capsule and our children will remain here. I don't think I have to remind you, but I'll say it anyway. Daimon Gate is an independent universe. It is the gateway between several universes, and the only way to travel for some. If you do anything against the Daimon Gate's rules, you are going against the multiverse," Ciaran said.

"The children are Daimon Gate guests now. It's against our rules for you or anyone else to attack them," Jennifer added.

"And you think I don't know that?" Moira said. "It has been a very long time since I've been here. I wouldn't mind visiting the current Host," Moira said.

Ciaran looked at Jennifer. Moira caught the look and continued, "I was the wife of the first King of Eudaiz. I didn't hold an official role in the council, but you can be certain that I accompanied Pierre to meet with the Host on several occasions."

"If Moira is eligible to see the Host, the entrance of the residence will open for her. If not, she will know she isn't welcome," Jennifer said dryly.

Ciaran nodded. He knew the drill. When they passed through the Daimon Gate for the first time, he'd had to fight for an invitation to see the Host. But now that he was the king-to-be of Eudaiz, and Madeline was his wife, he should have easy access to the Host's residence.

Moira smiled slightly and sauntered out of the capsule. Ciaran took Madeline's hand and led her outside. Jennifer glanced at the children's boxes and then turned on her heel, closing the capsule door behind her.

Outside, the air was misty. The sense of something strange intensified in the air, making Madeline shudder. Ciaran frowned at her reaction, but he didn't ask the reason for it. The aura of the surrounding area felt wrong to him as well. The air stirred, and the door of the entrance to the Host's residence appeared directly in front of them.

Moira smirked, striding straight to the door's control panel. She pressed her palm on the verificator. It identified her as Moira LeBlanc, and the door swung open.

"Left palm," Ciaran murmured.

In Eudaiz, only the king had left palm verification.

Madeline hissed. Moira was not only Ciaran's great ancestor but also someone as important as the first king of Eudaiz. She didn't need an official role to be recognized. She must be even more important than the King of Eudaiz and the council. If the Eudaizian people considered Sciphils their gods, this woman could possibly be the boss of their gods and goddesses. Yet Madeline had punched the woman in the head to knock her out. Madeline was sure her action had been called for in that particular situation, but the future consequences couldn't be pretty.

Ciaran's wrist unit flashed alarm red. Then a message ran across his screen. As he read it, the blood drained out of his face. "They've got Tadgh," he said.

"Who are *they?* What do they want?" Jennifer asked.

Ciaran contemplated. "He will be replacing the late Sciphil Seven. If the position isn't filled by tomorrow, we will lose the power of Tower Seven. Eudaiz will collapse as a result. Whoever took Tadgh wants to negotiate with me. They won't kill him. And they don't want Eudaiz to collapse because if they did, they would have killed him already."

"Was that message from them?" Madeline asked.

Ciaran shook his head. "I've turned off the communication channel of the wrist unit because I didn't want anyone to track us. No one in Eudaiz knows where we are now. That's for the safety of you and the children."

"It must be chaos now in Eudaiz. Tadgh was taken, and they couldn't find us. So who sent you the message?" Madeline said.

"A tracking device on Tadgh. It messages me when he's in danger and gives me his whereabouts."

"You bugged your brother?" Moira laughed.

"And where is he now?" Jennifer asked.

Ciaran looked at Madeline. "Black Rock. And no, you're not going with me, Madeline."

"No one in Eudaiz has ever set foot in Black Rock. You can't go on your own. You don't know what's there," Madeline said, tears gleaming in her eyes. But she knew he had made up his mind.

"Promise me you'll stay here for the children. Don't contact anyone in Eudaiz. I don't want anyone to find out where you are while I'm gone. Can you promise me that, Madeline?"

She nodded.

Ciaran said nothing but ran to Moira, grabbed her, and tied her up despite her physical and verbal protests. "I apologize for being rough with you. I've got no time, and you pose a potential threat to my family." Then he looked at Jennifer. "Mother, I'm going have to borrow a capsule."

Jennifer nodded and tossed Ciaran a small electronic keypad. "It's waiting right at the gate. Be careful, Son. I don't care to have the both of my sons hurt in the same day."

"Please help Madeline take care of the babies," Ciaran said.

Jennifer arched an eyebrow. "Do you have to ask?"

Ciaran nodded a thank you to his mother. Before he left, Madeline grabbed him and kissed him. He responded and embraced her, hanging on tightly for a moment. "I love you, Ciaran. Come back to me and the children."

"I will." He kissed her one more time and then ran toward the vehicle.

CHAPTER 34

Ciaran hovered the borrowed capsule low to the ground and maneuvered between rocks shaped like the devil's claws and fangs. He glanced at the monitor of his wrist unit and estimated his position compared to the tracker which showed his brother's whereabouts.

Black Rock was the sewer of the multiverse. That was Ciaran's observation. Calling it the universe of darkness was too glamorous. There was nothing here but waste. He felt sorry for its native creatures and understood why they attacked Eudaiz all the time to steal resources.

This was his firsthand impression of this universe, and he had an odd feeling that over the hundreds of years of battle, the Eudaizian citizens' impression that Black Rock was their number one enemy was wrong. This wasn't a combat-ready universe. The most it could do would be to provide soldiers for hire.

That meant their true number one enemy was unknown.

The tracker suggested he was very close to where Tadgh was captured. But in front of him was nothingness. Not even a large rock.

He glanced at the radar. It detected nothing.

Suddenly, the capsule slammed straight into something hard.

The capsule exploded. All Ciaran saw was a blinding flash.

***

In the Daimon Gate, Madeline opened her eyes and saw the ceiling of her children's chamber. She must have fainted, falling to the floor of the capsule.

Jennifer was arguing with Moira.

"What did you do to her?" Jennifer asked Moira.

"Nothing except for helping her to give birth to the children. My technology is a lot more advanced than that of Eudaiz. So whatever is happening isn't my doing."

Jennifer turned and grabbed Madeline's shoulders to shake her but saw that she had regained consciousness.

"Don't die on me, Madeline. I wouldn't want to see the look on Ciaran's face when he comes back and finds that he has to take care of the children himself."

Madeline sat up by herself, groggy. A tear rolled down her face.

She had just had a psychic episode and had seen Ciaran's capsule explode.

It wasn't a precognition because she *knew* it had happened.

She sat on the floor, leaning against the wall of her children's birth chamber. There were no more tears on her face, but her teeth started to chatter. She was hyperventilating, and her hands shook.

"What happened, Madeline?" Jennifer asked.

She couldn't speak. She knew she was going into shock. This was weak of her. She couldn't let it happen. Madeline looked at her shaky hands. She closed her eyes and concentrated.

The place was dark. The explosion was harsh. She replayed again what she had seen in her mind.

The explosion. Ciaran's shadow.

There was something about the explosion. It wasn't inside the capsule. Wasn't right outside it, either. It was more like a jolt of energy. She didn't know what it was. She couldn't make sense of what she had seen. But she could make sense of what she hadn't seen.

She hadn't seen Ciaran dead.

***

A cool hand brushed over the wound on his forehead woke Ciaran. He opened his eyes and saw a pale female face looking at him. It could be the beautiful face of a girl in her mid-twenties on Earth, but something in the girl's big sad eyes was so haunting it tugged at him. She was trying to take care of his injuries.

"What's your name?" he asked. He tried to move his hands but couldn't, and he figured they must be tied. The cold seeped into his skin, suggesting he was lying on some kind of rock.

She looked at him and said, "Libby." Her voice was hollow and distant.

She was a Black Rock creature.

Ciaran had never seen a Black Rock creature express so much emotion. So much sadness.

Libby tugged at the rope tying him as if to make sure it wasn't cutting into his skin. Then he felt an object being slid into his hand. He grabbed it.

The girl's head perked up at the footsteps of someone approaching. The sadness in the girl's eyes was replaced by fear.

Someone spoke in the native language. The girl said something back and earned a hard slap. She fell to the floor. A man shouted at the girl until she scurried outside.

Ciaran sat bolt upright and saw Kyle looming over him. Kyle smirked. "I never thought in my wildest dreams that I would have both of the LeBlanc brothers in my hands." He clucked his tongue. "I promised to hand you over alive. But I didn't promise I wouldn't hurt you."

Fast and fierce as a storm, Kyle grabbed Ciaran and flung him across the room. He crashed into furniture and a lot of hard objects unfriendly to his human body. He swore he could hear his bones rattle.

Ciaran could see his guns, daggers, and wrist unit on the table. But before he could make a run for them, Kyle darted over, picked him up from the floor, and zoomed across the room with him.

He pressed Ciaran's face hard against a decorative rock on the wall. On the black rock was a carving of a giant serpent wrapped around a boat.

"This is Black Rock—a land you shouldn't set foot in," Kyle snarled.

Ciaran said, "I understand you're scared of me. But how much satisfaction will you get beating me up like this? Untie me. We can do it one on one. You're the one with the supernatural power. Before my coronation, I am only a man. You see?"

Kyle laughed. "You want to stir up my ego? Unfortunately, I have let go of that since Bran exiled me from Eudaiz. Kyle threw him across the room. His body smashed into the wall. He didn't hear any bones rattle this time. Maybe there were none left intact.

Kyle picked him up again and squeezed his neck. "Beg! If you beg, I will spare you the pain, Ciaran."

Ciaran head-butted Kyle right onto his nose. Kyle roared.

Kyle threw him again—this time over a stone bench. He saw stars. Every cell in his body wanted to separate one from one another. Kyle flew over, grabbed him by his neck, and threw him to the opposite wall like a rag doll. He dropped in a heap at the bottom of the wall.

Kyle gave him a few more kicks before striding to an adjacent room to make a call.

Lying on the floor, Ciaran could hear Kyle's voice echoing back to the room. The person Kyle was talking to must be the one who wanted him and Tadgh captured. Whoever it was, Kyle spoke to him or her in English.

Kyle spat out some profanity and left the room after finishing the conversation. Ciaran lay still for a while to gather some of his human strength and then slid out the small object Libby had left him. It felt like a piece of metal. He started cutting the ropes binding his wrists.

Quickly, he freed himself. He took back his weapons and paused, looking at his wrist unit. The small piece of technology contained a massive amount of information about him. It could reveal psychological and biological profiles he didn't care for others to know about.

The person who had ordered Kyle to capture him wanted him alive and wanted this piece of technology, too. Someone wanted to know a lot about him—and maybe about Eudaiz as well.

Ciaran tracked Tadgh's current location and estimated they were in very close proximity, possibly in the same venue.

He sneaked the door open and saw a long and dark corridor.

Suddenly, footsteps approached, and the door opened wide. He jerked back.

CHAPTER 35

Libby stood in front of Ciaran with a keypad in her hand. She gestured at the corridor and led the way. Ciaran followed without asking questions. He wagered Libby had no reason to lead him to a trap.

They went down multiple levels in the dark dungeon. The stench of damp soil, mold, and some kind of black mud engulfed Ciaran. But Libby didn't seem to mind.

A small group of creatures with lizard heads and fox tails exited a small room along the corridor as they approached. Ciaran pushed Libby behind him and pulled his guns. Before the creatures could retaliate, their bodies copped several beams from

Ciaran's gun. They convulsed on the floor, turned into puddles of black liquid, and evaporated into thin air.

Libby raced toward the end of the corridor to a small, black, heavy-looking door. She tapped it. A small window opened from the inside, and a pair of eyes stared out. The conversation was carried out in a stream of native language, and Ciaran guessed that she was trying to get the other creature let her inside the room. He thought Tadgh was most likely in that little cell.

His prediction was correct.

Ciaran entered the room. The creature hadn't expected Ciaran. He glared at Libby, spat out some profanity in native language, pulled out a knife and rushed toward her. Ciaran grabbed the creature and, with a slight twist of his wrists, he broke the warden's neck. The creature dropped to the ground, wriggling in pain before it died, and its body evaporated into thin air.

Libby proceeded to another doorway and pulled at a heavy oak door. It squeaked open, revealing Tadgh inside, sitting on the floor, chained to the wall.

Ciaran rushed over. "He's not conscious. Do you have the key for the chain?"

Ciaran looked at Libby. To answer his series of questions, Libby just shook her head.

"All right, I'm going to beam this." Ciaran pulled his gun and nudged Libby aside.

Tadgh groggily opened his eyes. "Ciaran!"

Ciaran said, "Are you okay? How bad did Kyle beat you up? Do you think there's any internal bleeding? There isn't much I can do here. We have to get you back to Eudaiz." Ciaran checked Tadgh's pulse.

Tadgh yanked his wrist out of Ciaran's hand. "I'm okay. But you look like shit, big brother!"

"Thank you for the compliment. I'm sure you spent your last moments thinking about my pretty face," Ciaran said and signaled Tadgh to look away. He fired at the lock on the chain. In a couple of shots, the lock melted and gave way. Ciaran helped Tadgh stand up.

"Are you okay, Libby?" Tadgh stretched his legs.

"Look like you know each other. Let's get out of here," Ciaran said.

"I just know her name. She helped me when the son of the bitch pounded on me," Tadgh said. Then he narrowed his eyes. He grabbed Libby's chin, tilted her face up, and stared at her bruised forehead. "Kyle beat you, too?"

"Yes. Because she tried to help me. You do realize that she's a Black Rock creature without much grasp of English, Tadgh? Let's get out of here before we get caught again."

"I'll make him pay ten times," Tadgh muttered and strode out of the cell.

Libby led them through dark corridors that appeared to be abandoned. At the end of the corridor, she reached a small door. She looked at Ciaran, gesturing for his gun.

Ciaran nodded. He beamed at the lock.

Ciaran's and Tadgh's jaws dropped. In front of them was what appeared to be a capsule park. It was much like the parking lots on Earth. The capsules were all private size, and Ciaran could only hope they hadn't been equipped for combat. If so, Eudaizian civilian areas wouldn't stand a chance.

From inside the premises, a group of vampirish creatures charged at them, fangs bared. Saying nothing, Ciaran pulled his guns and sprayed in their direction. In no time, he had cleared up the pursuit.

"We'd better hurry—there will be more of them," Tadgh warned.

Libby held up a keypad. She ran across the park. Light flashed from a capsule the size of a four-seat car. Unlike Eudaiz, where everything was computerized and centralized, this one was a private vehicle with a private lock. Just like the old-fashioned way on Earth.

Libby gave the key to Ciaran, then she stepped back and gestured at the door.

"You're going with us, Libby," Ciaran told her.

She shook her head.

"You can't go back in. He'll kill you, Libby," Tadgh said and tugged Libby's elbow to nudge her into the capsule. She jerked back.

"Go," Libby said.

"We can't leave you here," Ciaran said.

Libby shook her head again. "Go!" she said.

"I hate to force a lady, but sometimes a man has to incur wrath in doing so," Tadgh muttered. He scooped Libby up and carried her into the capsule. He jumped in to lock the way out. Ciaran slid into the driver's seat as if it had been made for him.

"Are you sure you can drive this thing?" Tadgh asked. While Ciaran loved speed, Tadgh had severe tachophobia. Apparently, Eudaizian energy hadn't cured his brother's fear of speed. Ciaran raised an eyebrow at his question.

"Sorry. Of course. You can drive anything that has an engine and a steering wheel," Tadgh muttered.

Libby wriggled out of Tadgh's hold and cried out loud. "Leave me," she said.

"I'm afraid we can't. You saved us. We can't sit back and let you be killed," Ciaran said.

"There are others!" Libby cried.

"You mean your family?" Tadgh asked.

Libby shook her head.

"Dead," she mangled out the word.

"You family is dead?" Ciaran asked.

She nodded.

"So why do you want to stay here?" Tadgh asked.

"Others," she said.

"You mean there are other girls like you here?" Ciaran asked.

Libby nodded. Her pale skin had become paler, almost gray. Tears rolled down her face. It surprised Ciaran that her tears were like human tears. Clear. Huge tears rolled out from the girl's sad eyes.

"All right, if we take the other girls as well, will you leave with us?" Ciaran asked.

Tadgh grinned. "We can certainly squeeze a few more of her friends in here. Let's go kick those bloody Black Rock asses," Tadgh said.

"Where to?" Ciaran asked and gestured toward the navigational board. Libby reached up from her seat and typed in the address. 'KHANUILAY.'

Ciaran started the engine. The capsule came to life, moved up and hovered a moment, and then zoomed in the direction he assumed led to a place called Khanuilay.

CHAPTER 36

In the distance, they could see Khanuilay at the bottom of a black stone quarry. Rock walls and cliffs surrounded three square black structures like a prison without the fences.

There were no creatures.

There was no sound.

The atmosphere was as eerie as that of a tomb.

Libby scurried toward a small rock and pressed it. It slid aside, revealing a door. Ciaran and Tadgh followed her inside.

They followed a small tunnel, heading downward. The surface of the wall of the tunnel was rough. It appeared to have been carved using hand tools rather than any technology. There was no light. Libby moved on ahead. Ciaran turned on a small light on his wrist unit to shed some light into the tunnel.

"Why don't you have a weapon on you? Nothing. Not even your wrist unit, Tadgh? If my tracker hadn't been inside your belt, how would anyone in Eudaiz have found you?" Ciaran asked.

"I was in training."

"What sort of training was Sciphil Nine giving you that didn't involve weapons?" Ciaran asked.

"Mediation!"

Silence.

"All right. I was in training, but I thought I'd sneak out to give Jo a call using my private communicator," Tadgh said.

"So you must have dropped it when Kyle took you. Everyone in Eudaiz thinks you're in training now. Am I correct?"

"Apparently . . . Man, we are going down deep . . . to those prison-like buildings," Tadgh muttered.

"It looks like a concentration camp to me," Ciaran said.

Libby arrived at a door and tapped it three times. The door was opened from the other side.

Tadgh's eyes widened. "You're right, Ciaran. *Shit.* Is this really a concentration camp?"

There must have been more than two hundred people in those square, cold bunkers. Flickering dim lighting. Poor ventilation. All wore identical gray clothes that made prisoners' uniform look glamorous and comfortable.

They stood up, watching as Libby stepped inside with Ciaran and Tadgh.

Hundreds of pairs of eyes. Hollow eyes even sadder than Libby's.

But behind the eyes, the dull gray skin, and the zombie-like movements, they were actually quite beautiful. Ciaran frowned.

"Something strike you as familiar here, Tadgh?" Ciaran asked between his teeth.

"Yep. But I dare not think about it. I'm not sure. But one thing I do know for sure—we can't fit them all into our capsule."

Ciaran looked closer at a couple of people approaching Libby now. Their shape. The way they looked at him. The way they conducted themselves. If he wasn't mistaken, they had once been Eudaizians.

Libby said something to them. They looked at him and Tadgh. They signaled others. And then they approached Ciaran and Tadgh, still keeping a distance. Some of them bowed.

An old man approached Ciaran and said, "Home. We miss home."

"Holy shit. They really *are* who we think they are," Tadgh spoke between his teeth. "How can we get them out of here?"

"I'll return to Eudaiz and gather the troops," Ciaran told them. "I'll come back, and I'll bring you home."

Some of them had tears in their eyes. Some cried out loud.

"We should leave now," Ciaran said. "Would you take us back to the capsule?"

Libby nodded.

Something landed next to the bunker and exploded, punching a hole in the wall.

"Leave! Now!" the old who had just spoken to Ciaran shouted. Libby led Ciaran and Tadgh back to the tunnel, and the people inside the bunker slammed it closed.

Libby charged ahead. Tears streamed down her face.

Tadgh stopped and looked back at the bunker.

"Leave now, Tadgh. There will be troops out there. We only add two casualties, nothing more," Ciaran said and followed Libby. Tadgh trailed behind.

More explosions shook the tunnel, loosening dirt and rock which rained down on them as they ran. They reached the top of the hill and charged for their capsule. From up there, they could see a sea of Black Rock soldiers surrounding the bunkers. Most of them seemed to lurk around the outside building, but a couple of them entered.

Then there was chaos. Squealing and screaming from inside the bunkers.

Above them, they heard a hideous quack. They looked up and saw a bird-like creature. It flapped its wings and squawked again at them. When it flew directly at them, Ciaran pulled his guns and fired. Its head exploded. The beams from the guns were quiet, but the creature's noises had alerted the troops at the bottom of the quarry.

They lined up and pulled their weapons. Tadgh looked down. "Cannons! Man, is it the medieval ages here?"

A cannonball landed nearby and exploded, tossing Tadgh, Ciaran, and Libby several feet away onto the rocky ground.

"To the capsule!" Ciaran yelled. A volley of cannonballs hit the surrounding area. Soon they would hit the capsule. More of the monstrous birds approached. Ciaran shot them. Still more flew in to take their place.

Soon there would be more than two guns could handle.

A loud bang echoed up the hill.

Then more bangs.

The ex-Eudaizians stormed out of the bunkers and attacked the troops at the bottom of the quarry.

The soldiers fired at the civilians. But the civilians fearlessly advanced.

The cannon fire at the top of the hill stopped.

Ciaran took out the rest of the birds.

Quiet reigned.

Libby stared down. Tears streamed down her face.

At the bottom of the quarry, the bodies of the Black Rock creatures began to disintegrate and evaporate.

The bodies of the dead Eudaizians, however, returned to their normal skin tone and did not disappear.

"I'm going with you," Libby said.

Tadgh said nothing and scooped Libby into the capsule. Ciaran drove away.

They entered the Eudaizian zone, and Ciaran's wrist unit beeped several times when their capsule was verified. He knew that, without the verification, entering Eudaiz from the Black Rock zone would be a deadly mistake.

Libby bent forward in her seat and gasped.

"Stop the capsule, Ciaran. Stop!" Tadgh shouted. As soon as Ciaran stopped, Libby rushed out of the capsule. She fell to the ground, gasping for air. Tadgh gathered her into his arms. "Tell me what you need, Libby," he said.

"You can't handle Eudaiz's air, can you? If I take you to the medical center, would it help?" Ciaran asked.

Libby shook her head. She was fading away, her eyes glassing over.

"No, no, there has to be a way. Tell me, Libby!" Tadgh shook her.

Libby's skin started to return to the milky tone of a Eudaizian. Her dark hair turned sandy white, her eyes glowed blue. She was as beautiful as an angel. She whispered, "Thank you for bringing me home. They captured us. They've turned us. I can't live as a Eudaizian. But I can die one . . ."

She smiled weakly and turned aside. She saw a small blue rock on the ground. "I'll take that. I'll be in there. Promise me ... you'll bring the bodies at the camp home. So ... they can ... at peace . . ." She drew in her last breath and died. Her body glowed and then gradually disintegrated and vanished. The blue rock she had pointed to flashed once and returned to its previous stage.

Tears rolled down Tadgh's face. He picked up the rock and slid it into his pocket.

CHAPTER 37

Kyle roared in anger and swung his sword. The head of the creature that used to be his messenger dropped to the floor and rolled into the corner. Dark blood spurted onto the ceilings.

"Get out of my sight," he screamed.

The three other creatures in the room raced outside.

Once alone in the dark dungeon where he'd tied Tadgh up, Kyle shook his head and smiled to himself. He was very pleased with the result of his little stunt at the Khanuilay camp. He knew his time was coming. The tide was turning in his favor.

Those little pawns running away now would spread the rumor. Any lingering Eudaizian spies in Black Rock would take that as breaking news. "Kyle is furious because his captives got away . . ." he mocked the expired Black Rock creature and laughed. But Kyle didn't think Eudaiz would have spies here. It was contrary to the Eudaizian code of ethics to do something like that.

He couldn't believe the LeBlanc brothers had fallen for his trap so easily. The cost of a few hundred Eudaizian prisoners wasn't high at all. After all, they were so stubborn that even after being converted, they wouldn't fight as soldiers.

He strode out of the basement and back to his black stone office. He opened a small compartment tucked away behind a black stone sculpture and took out a small stone, half the size of his palm. The stone glowed a shade of pale emerald.

He rubbed his thumb on the stone. "Chiara, I'm sorry about Libby. But something had to give. If you don't like what you see, maybe you should have thought more carefully before you rejected me."

He kissed the stone and put it back into the compartment.

***

Madeline walked back and forth in the children's chamber, occasionally glancing at the two square boxes she'd been told were her children. She wanted to hit something. Shout at someone. Her agitation wasn't a good sign.

She could no longer feel Ciaran. She knew something had happened. If only she could feel him, she could help him. But an attempt to reach out might leak the signal and reveal her location. That would defeat the purpose of Ciaran's plans to keep her and the children safe.

Her mother in law, Jennifer, had taken Moira, her wicked five-hundred-year-old ancestor, inside the residence. She should go in to talk to her father-in-law. But she couldn't bring herself to do it.

Something felt really wrong. She didn't know what it was. Her psychic ability was useless outside Eudaiz. She needed to practice more.

She walked around for a little more and recalled the sign she'd seen on the garden wall—*Ennead will kill you all*. Ciaran and she had solved that puzzle during her officiation. But given that Kyle had made such a huge deal out of it, it couldn't be possible that she had solved it once and for all. A guy like

Kyle who held a grudge for more than thirty years wouldn't let go that easily.

Ciaran said Kyle wouldn't be able to pull the ennead stunt by himself.

Who was he working with? What if there was another decoding session of the ennead? Last time, Ciaran said he wasn't prepared, and they would have lost if it hadn't been for her psychic ability. She had connected with and read the mind of the coder, and she'd heard him screaming out the answer in his mind.

But this time, Ciaran was with Tadgh, and Tadgh was a number genius, not a psychic.

Tadgh was an emotional guy, and the fact that after an incident on Earth, he had developed an ability to read emotions didn't help him at all.

Most importantly, none of that would help with decoding the ennead if it were required this time.

What would it be?

Madeline closed her eyes and concentrated to see if she could get a signal of anyone or anything related to this matter.

Nothing.

She tried again.

Nothing.

Then a beam of light flashed down from the ceiling in front of her. The cone of light was haloed by a mysterious blue glow. Her psychic ability always began with her seeing blue dots—the minds of others. But there had never been anything like this. Whose mind was this that she was seeing?

She reached her hand out and touched the light. The suction was incredible. She was drawn into a holospace of weightlessness, full of light beams flashing in different dimensions.

When her feet touched the ground, she reached her hand out again—and touched the cold, smooth surface of thin air! How could that be? She pushed. Her hand touched the smooth, hard surface again.

It felt like the surface of a mirror. But she was sure it was only the air in front of her. The flashing blue light made it difficult for her to see much. But if there were a mirror in front of her, then she would see her reflection. She pushed as if she was about to walk into that empty space.

Something swung, and she was flipped over to a different space. The light beams in here were deep red, swirling around as if she were in a night club, minus the music and the dancing.

Not wanting to hit her face against a hard surface, she reached out her hand to touch that smooth surface again. This time, something zapped her hand. It felt like an electric shock. She jerked back and fell into a wall behind her, which flipped her a different room.

She fell onto a cold steel floor. She looked down. It wasn't steel at all. It was a mirrored floor.

Deep down inside the mirror, she saw the emerald glow of a stone. The stone blinked at her as if wanting to communicate with her. She felt an odd connection to the stone. Like someone was watching her from below. Someone she knew.

She was scrambling in someone's mind. A massive mind. Or maybe the tangled minds of those related to her. And this was a mirror maze.

Deception.

That was all she could think of.

She stood up, staggered back. She closed her eyes and made herself fall out of the psychic episode.

CHAPTER 38

Tadgh prowled around like a hungry lion looking for a kill. Ciaran had never seen Tadgh this angry. His brother was always impulsive and emotional, but he didn't think Tadgh had that much fury in him.

When it came to fury, Ciaran knew what it was like. His own rage was primal and maybe the worst in the cosmos. He could kill with a mere thought when he was angry enough. And he had done that.

A message came across Ciaran's wrist unit, reporting that the officiation for Sciphil Seven was ready. Ciaran and Tadgh got into the capsule and transported themselves to Tower Seven.

The outside structure of Tower Seven was identical to that of Tower One—round, imposing, and mysterious. The gray structure peered down at them as they approached. Ciaran verified his palm print, and the door slid open.

The walked through nine layers of thick steel walls. The rotating nine walls would grind a trespasser into dust.

The grand hallway opened to them, leading them to the center of the tower where the control room and officiation chamber were located. Lights illuminated as they walked past.

Similar to the chamber used for Madeline's officiation, Tower Seven's round glass chamber was inviting. Acting on what had happened to Madeline, Ciaran gestured Tadgh to stop.

"I need to use the computer for a bit before you get in there," Ciaran said.

"All right, I'll wait."

"Actually, you could help me with this." Tadgh was a math and matrix genius, a walking, talking computer when it came to solving mathematical problems. "In a nutshell, we have a mole in our executives. Whoever it is interfered with the system and forced a replacement of one source of energy. When we officiated Madeline for Sciphil One position, the computer asked us to verify two layers of codes to accept the alternative energy."

"You think it might ask again?"

Ciaran nodded. "It was referred to as the ennead code. I speculated it was the nine Gods in Egyptian mythology. The top of the family line was Atum. That was the god who created the ennead. So I got that one right. But I didn't guess the second level."

"Madeline guessed it?" Tadgh raised an eyebrow.

"She was presented with nine names of pyramids and asked to choose one. Each choice would result in the collapse of a dimension. Choosing the wrong one could lead to the destruction of a dimension we care about—such as Earth."

"Did she use her psychic ability?"

Ciaran nodded. "And psychic ability is what you and I don't have. You can read emotions these days, but I don't think it will help much in this case."

"Do you remember the second level choices?"

"I think level one will stay the same, but I'm sure level two will change," Ciaran said and walked toward the computer. He searched for the information about the ennead. He continued, "Atum is the father and on top of his family tree. Madeline's position is Sciphil One, so I speculated the code was Atum. Yours is Sciphil Seven. I wager the code would be the third generation of Atum family tree and number seven, Isis."

Tadgh shoved his hands in his pocket and walked around. As Ciaran had predicted, Tadgh was intrigued by the problem.

"But you're unsure?" Tadgh asked.

"I have never been sure about this. My knowledge of Egyptian mythology is quite limited."

"But you got Atum right!"

Ciaran shook his head. "What if I get it wrong this time?"

Tadgh shrugged. "We don't have any more time, do we?"

Before Ciaran could answer, his unit flashed a message from Sizx, "The network is connected. Countdown has started."

"I guess I should go in. Game on," Tadgh said and walked toward the tall glass chamber in the middle of the room.

Ciaran glanced at his brother and saw that Tadgh had deliberately focused his attention on the keyboard inside the glass chamber. He didn't return Ciaran's look. Ciaran activated the process on his control panel. The door of the glass chamber sealed.

Similar to Madeline's Sciphil One officiation, the round circle of light beamed down to Tadgh, and a thousand beams of white and blue light washed over him.

Ciaran could feel every nerve in him quivering. He couldn't let his anxiety cloud his judgment.

The process was almost complete. Tadgh glowed under a halo of blue energy. Ciaran smiled. His little brother would make a magnificent warrior and an excellent Sciphil Seven.

The spin of light slowed to a halt, and a message appeared on the screen. The one Ciaran had been worrying about.

"An energy source has been corrupted and was replaced. Please confirm your acceptance of the alternate energy. Enter the ennead code." The text blinked at Tadgh. Tadgh looked at Ciaran for a last confirmation and entered the code.

CHAPTER 39

Madeline paced back and forth in the children's chamber. Her agitation had intensified. She needed to tell Ciaran about her psychic episode. It might not be just a psychic episode but a precognition. She needed to know if he was okay. She needed to talk to Ciaran. He could make a lot more sense out of her psychic vision than she could.

But she couldn't engage his wrist unit. He had said so. If she did, the communication would reveal her current location and make her and the children vulnerable to attack.

***

In Eudaiz, at Tower Seven, Tadgh stared at the computer monitor and the flashing question for the ennead code. He looked at Ciaran pacing around and around the glass chamber like a lion. He knew his big brother would storm in here and pick at this puzzle himself if he could.

Sometimes Ciaran worried too much about him. But it was partially his own fault. He had always appeared immature, and he knew that. But now, at this moment, the matter was in his hands, and there was nothing Ciaran could do.

Ciaran had said a wrong choice would lead to death. But hell, if he were to take on the Sciphil Seven position and be responsible for the life of those millions of people, this small sacrifice, should it happen, wouldn't be a big deal.

Tadgh held his breath and typed *Isis* into the code box.

The screen blinked, and a line of text appeared, "Success. Level confirmed."

Tadgh looked at Ciaran and almost snorted when he saw the relief on his brother's face. Then the screen flashed the second level question. It was no surprise to them. The computer presented Tadgh with nine options and asked which dimension he would collapse to compensate for his alternate energy.

Regardless of the polished way Ciaran had put it, it was the same as asking which universe Tadgh would kill to save his life and the lives of the citizens in District Seven. If he got it right, someone else in the cosmos would die. If he got it wrong, he and several million people in District Seven would perish.

This was a huge life change from the days he'd been enjoying a good life on Earth, traveling extensively, and totally carefree.

Tadgh stared at the nine options available to him on the screen, and his eyes immediately glued to one—KHANUILAY. The name of the camp where the Eudaizians had been imprisoned.

***

Madeline stared at her wrist unit, her finger hovering close to the engage button. Something terribly wrong was going to happen, and she needed to call her husband.

***

In the living quarters of his residence, Kyle leaned back in a large armchair, drunk. The emerald stone of Chiara was on the table, staring at him. Judging him?

He sat straight up, talking to the stone, "You're not judging me, are you?" He reached for his wine, a special red wine he made for his own consumption. It kept his spirits up. Traditional rich red wine mixed with blood. Blood from human innocents made the best wine. But given he was in Black Rock now, he couldn't afford such luxury.

He got by with blood from Black Rock creatures. Or any creatures he captured.

He called them expendable objects. No sense confusing them with those he couldn't afford to kill such as the LeBlancs.

The wine calmed him. He was in a celebratory mood. Very shortly, Tadgh would enter a wrong choice, and Kyle would have his way in this matter.

He chuckled and raised the glass in a toast to the air, congratulating himself.

CHAPTER 40

His blood was boiling. Tadgh could feel it. Nine options on the computer screen blinked at him, but he could see only one. Khanuilay. The scene of the dead bodies of innocent Eudaizian captives piling up after an attempt to save them enraged Tadgh.

Those people had no defense. No life. And no hope left in them. Because Ciaran and Tadgh had come from Eudaiz, those people had been willing to sacrifice themselves with only a slim hope that Ciaran could escape back to Eudaiz and return to free them.

It was the same with Libby. They knew their right to be Eudaizian had been stolen from them. All they could do to be Eudaizian again was die.

Who were the Black Rock? Who was Kyle and whoever it was in charge of this plot? Who were they to play with that many innocent lives? Tadgh asked the questions, knowing he wouldn't be able to find any answers.

But it was a no brainer for him now. The choice he would make was Khanuilay. Those innocents had died. If he chose Khanuilay as the target dimension to destroy, they would destroy Black Rock. And that would solve hundreds of years of problems for Eudaiz.

He looked at Ciaran and said, "I'm going to choose Khanuilay."

"No," Ciaran said.

"Why?"

"It would be too . . . convenient."

"After what happened in Black Rock? After how many people died? You still think someone planned all this, Ciaran?"

"I'm not sure yet!"

"We don't have time. This is our one and only chance to destroy Black Rock. I'm willing to pay for whatever it costs to take them down."

"But I'm not willing to pay that price, Tadgh. Give me one moment to think," Ciaran said and looked at the options again. Tadgh rocked back and forth on his heels, waiting impatiently.

***

In the children's chamber, Madeline turned to look at her babies. Still in those square boxes. Still relying on her protection. Still innocent.

When was the last time she'd used her psychic ability to communicate with Ciaran? The first time, it was at the creek down the hill at his home in Henley-on-Thames, England. It was a one-way communication. In her mind, she had asked him to think of her so she could track his thoughts and find him. He did. But he didn't have psychic ability, and he couldn't read her thoughts.

The second time was when he was forced to train across different dimensions and was almost killed. She had reached out to his mind and communicated with him in his subconscious. But that had required physical contact between them.

Now, in this situation, she had no idea what to do.

***

Ciaran stared at the other eight options on the screen. The options were Sekhmet, Ra, Hathor, Thoth, Anubis, Amun, Apep, and Bastet. Aside from Khanuilay, a location from Black Rock, the other eight were Egyptian gods.

He wasn't sure. He didn't know the answer.

But he couldn't make a decision on a gut feeling.

He needed his wife. Ciaran closed his eyes and concentrated. He didn't have the psychic ability. Madeline did. And after her officiation, her ability was a lot stronger. In his mind, he reached out for her.

He searched in the darkness.

Nothing. No sound. No images.

Then he saw it. It was light. A flash of light at the end of a tunnel. Traces of light. Traces of her energy. Images of her thoughts. He was sure of it. Blue light. Yellow. Flashing. And then a dim green light. The green halo flashed. Flashed. And flashed again.

He heard the faint echo of her voice calling out to him. "Emerald." That was what she said.

"Emerald," Ciaran said out loud and opened his eyes.

"Emerald isn't a choice," Tadgh said.

Ciaran walked over to the computer, which was flashing a countdown at him. He searched for emerald, colors, meaning, Egyptian gods . . . anything that might help. His eyes focused on a particular spot on the screen flowing with a river of data.

"There you are," Ciaran muttered and zoomed in on the data zone. Then he said to Tadgh, "Whatever you do, do *not* choose Khanuilay."

"So which one should I choose?" Tadgh asked.

Ciaran looked at the options again and contemplated. Then he recalled the carving on the black stone that Kyle had smashed his face against—the carving of a giant serpent. His fingers flew over the keyboard again. He looked at his brother and asked, "Tadgh, do you trust me?"

"Do I have a choice? It's counting down. Hurry."

The countdown had reach three.

"Apep," Ciaran said. Tadgh typed it on the computer keyboard just before the countdown reached zero.

A line of text flashed on the screen. "Verification successful. Congratulations, and welcome Sciphil Seven, Tadgh LeBlanc."

Tadgh paused. He stared in disbelief at the text, then he grinned. The door of the glass chamber slid open, and he walked out.

Ciaran slid down to the floor, exhausted.

He noted that he had consumed whatever natural energy Moira, his ancestor, had given him. He pulled out the reserve energy patch Sizx had given him in the morning and slapped it on his wrist.

"How did you know the answer?" Tadgh asked.

"I think Madeline tried to reach my subconscious. She said 'emerald.' When Libby died, it seemed like her essence was absorbed into the blue stone you still have in your pocket. I narrowed the search to Madeline's family. The database suggests that her mother, Chiara Kelly, was absorbed into an emerald stone when she died."

Tadgh took the blue stone out of his pocket and looked at it.

Ciaran continued, "Chiara used to live in a small village called Khanuilay in District One. The data suggests that village collapsed, and the village people all vanished, presumed dead. You and I know what happened to them. So effectively, if you chose Khanuilay, you would have destroyed millions of lives in District One. I'm not even sure Eudaiz could survive that kind of impact. The Khanuilay camp in Black Rock was merely a token name."

"Genius," Tadgh muttered.

"Or not," Ciaran said. "I think the person who captured the Eudaizians wasn't Kyle. But Kyle used the information. And if he were such a genius, he wouldn't have smashed my face against a carving of a giant serpent wrapping around a boat. That's a symbol of Apep, the god he worships."

Tadgh nodded. "Wow. What a process, Ciaran. What now?"

Ciaran shook his head, trying to shake away his fatigue. "You will have to handle the process of media releases. There are politics to deal with. I have to get back to Madeline. She's in the Daimon Gate now with the children. Don't mention that info on any communication device."

"You? Madeline? The children?" Tadgh stuttered. "What?"

"Long story. I'll explain when things settle. I have to go now. And remember, no mention of our whereabouts to anyone before I say so."

"Okay. When will I get to see the children?"

"Soon," Ciaran said and strode out.

CHAPTER 41

Ciaran drove the capsule they stole from Black Rock. It probably wasn't a good idea, but he had limited options. It might be good in a way because the Eudaizian system wouldn't be able to trace this capsule.

Or maybe they'd identify it as a potential target . . .

Just as the thought crossed his mind, a missile hit his little capsule.

Ciaran fell into a hole of weightlessness. The air was thin, and there was no light. His body was flung out of the funnel-like hole in the ground like a cannonball. He flopped to the ground in a place that felt somewhat familiar. Then he couldn't remember anything else.

When he came to, he jumped quickly to his feet, but his body swayed. It was still dark. He couldn't get his bearings.

The ejection mechanism of the capsule must have shot him out when the capsule was struck.

He shook his head, but he couldn't see much. His mind was numb. He didn't know how long he had been lying there.

"Ciaran."

He shrugged off whoever was trying to grab him.

"Ciaran, Look at me, Ciaran."

He felt the warm trickle of flowing blood on his side and reached for his wound. He was too dazed to feel or see anything.

"Ciaran, look at me."

Ciaran was snapped back to reality. In front of him stood Sizx. She wore—if he was not mistaken—her pajamas.

Ciaran glanced around, breathing heavily and trying to draw in as much air as possible.

"Where am I?"

"Outside District Six."

So his capsule was indeed shot down because it was a Black Rock capsule. How stupid it was of him to drive it. Now here he was, running out of energy. He would be most likely be passing out any minute. Ciaran could feel his eyes threatening to roll back. He was leaking energy along with his blood. He wanted to flop to the ground, but he shook his head and forced himself to stay alert.

Madeline was still in the Daimon Gate. He had to get back to his wife and his children. He didn't know how now as his capsule had been shot down. The thought slashed at his heart and cut through his mind. His energy was much too low for his brain to function properly.

"I need your energy patch," Ciaran said.

"It's in my capsule."

Ciaran nodded. His body swayed again. Sizx slid her arm around his waist. "Let's get you inside. There's more air in there." Once inside, she said, "Promise me you'll let me take care of your injury." She cast a concerned look at Ciaran's side. He nodded and snatched the energy patch she held in her hand. He snapped it on and gave it a moment to work. Moira had given him back his natural energy, so now the artificial energy was functioning at its best.

Sizx fetched the medical kit and fumbled with it.

"How did you know I'd be outside District Six?" Ciaran took his shirt off.

Sizx wiped the blood away, cleaned the wound, and secured a bandage over it. She looked up at him and smiled. She had such a gracious smile, he thought. In response to Ciaran's question, Sizx picked up his shirt, flipped the inside of its lapel out, and peeled off a sticky plastic strip the size of a small button.

"You tagged me?" Ciaran exclaimed.

"Sorry. The morning your mother visited and I lent you the energy patch, I stuck that on you. It only signals me when you're where you are not supposed to be—such as outside the secured zone of District Six."

"So it tracks where I've been?" Ciaran narrowed his eyes.

Sizx shook her head. "No. It only works in this dimension. Have you traveled outside Eudaiz?"

Ciaran shook his head. "Did it ever occur to you that what you did violated my privacy?"

"No, it was for your safety." Sizx stared blankly at Ciaran. "If I had to, I'd put surveillance on everyone and everything in Eudaiz in order to maintain security. That's my job."

Ciaran jammed his hands into his pockets and contemplated whether he should ignore Sizx or bash her head against the dashboard to knock some sense into her and teach her some common Earth courtesy. Because he was a gentleman and didn't approve of violence against women, he decided on the first option. But that option didn't feel quite right, either. Ciaran had borrowed Sizx's energy patch—again—and was now plotting to borrow her private capsule to get back to the Daimon Gate and Xiilok. He thought that using his authoritative tone would not be a wise move.

"Why are you out and about at this hour—and in that outfit?" Ciaran asked.

"I should ask you the same question. This is District Six—I live here. I was about to turn in for the night when the spy bug signaled you were outside the boundary of District Six. As you haven't been to this district, you own no private capsule, and you have nothing official to do now in this district, I took the signal to be one of distress. As far as this outfit is concerned, I wear it to bed."

Ciaran looked at the woman—magnificent blue hair, perfect face and body, intelligent, and somehow utterly innocent aside from possessing the dark edges of something he hadn't quite figured out yet.

Ciaran cleared his throat. "I need to borrow your private capsule, Sizx."

"For private business, I would guess, because the official capsule system is far superior to my pitiful private transportation."

Ciaran nodded. "Yes. It's for private business. I'm asking you for another favor."

Sizx smiled. "You can't expect me to walk home in pajamas in the middle of the night."

Ciaran chuckled. "Of course not. I'll take you home first. I'd appreciate it if—"

"I would be discreet about this private business of yours?" she interjected.

Ciaran nodded and turned to start the capsule. Nothing happened. Sizx grinned. "It's a private capsule. You can drive it, but I need to verify in order for it to start. Let's go." She started the capsule, programmed the map, and let it auto drive.

"So I can't use the capsule without you?"

"No, not normally. But I can fix it so you can. I'll log into the system at my place and change the registration to authorize your access. It won't take long."

Ciaran nodded. "Thank you. I appreciate it, Sizx."

***

They arrived at Sizx's residence. *It looks very much like a contemporary apartment in London,* Ciaran mused. She verified at the door and let him in. *Small, cozy, and feminine,* Ciaran thought when he passed through the doorway into the living room.

Sizx gestured to the computer sitting in a corner of the room. She started it up and typed in her information. Ciaran looked at the screen as she worked. "What's your last name?" he asked.

"I don't have one. Like most other children in Eudaiz, I was born in a box. But unlike the others, whoever created me never claimed me."

Ciaran felt a sudden rush of sadness. Madeline had been dumped into a basket at four weeks of age, and Sizx had been shoved into a box and left to claw her way out. He thought about his own children and wondered how they were surviving in those boxes in the Daimon Gate.

"There, you're in," Sizx said when she finished the authorization.

"Thank you again. I owe you more than I can say. I have no idea know how to repay you. If you need anything in the future, just let me know."

Sizx looked at Ciaran. "Really?"

"Yes, of course. You have my word."

"I . . . never mind." She turned away.

"What's wrong?" Ciaran spun her around and looked into those big blue eyes. He could see some emotions stirring in there, but he knew she wouldn't care to admit them, so he let it pass.

"I've never been with a man before."

"I beg your pardon? I mean, I heard you, but why are you telling me that? What do you expect me to do?"

"I don't understand." She frowned.

"I'm not only married to Madeline, but I love her and my family more than I love my life. There is no room in me for anyone else."

"I'm not asking for your love."

"But Sizx . . . There's no time for me to explain it to you right now . . ."

She dropped her pajamas to the floor and stood in front of Ciaran, naked. Her flawless body glowed in the dim light of the living room, her blue eyes sparkled with desire, and her magnificent blue hair swirled around her shoulders invitingly.

"I'm flattered, Sizx. I really am. But a beautiful and intelligent woman like you deserves a lot better than an affair with a married man like me. You can have much better. Do you understand that?"

She stared at him and said, "No."

"If you keep this up, I will have to walk out of here without your capsule and your energy patch. In fact, I think I should give them back to you." Ciaran reached for the energy patch.

"Please don't." Sizx withdrew a step. A tear rolled from her eye and dropped onto her cheek. She wiped it with her finger. She stared at the teardrop and looked up at Ciaran. "I'm not asking for your love," she repeated. "I know what it is, in theory, and I know I won't ever have it from you. But this body is yours to take if you wish. All I ask from you is a kiss before I die—and that you let my essence absorb into a button of your shirt."

"A button of my shirt?"

"Every Eudaizian must indicate where they want to place their essence when they die. I don't want to be in a stone like everyone else. I don't want to be in a chapel. I have no family. No one will miss me. A button is an insignificant request, don't you think?"

She stood firm and looked him straight in the eye—and she was still naked.

"I... I don't know what to say," Ciaran stuttered, still managing to sound calm and composed.

"A kiss and a button. That's all I want."

Ciaran wanted to embrace her and smooth out all of her rough edges—it pained him to see her that way—but he didn't want his intentions to be misconstrued. So he let the thought pass. Ciaran nodded. "I promise."

"You should go now." Sizx looked down at the floor.

Ciaran admired the beautiful woman in front of him for a short moment and left quickly before she looked up.

CHAPTER 42

The fire had burned the ground, and it made the dark floor even darker. Kyle's body sprawled across a burning pool of liquid, looking like the blood of the creatures in his house. There was nothing surrounding him that could be called a house.

When he betrayed Eudaiz for Black Rock, they gave him the land that he called Apep, the name of his god. There was no God in Eudaiz. People lived such happy lives they didn't need to pray to God. But he had a god. He had a belief. And now his choice had become a curse that killed him.

He didn't understand how his plan could have gone so wrong.

He clutched the piece of emerald stone in his hand. The moment he felt his soul was leaving his body, he thought about Chiara again.

He still didn't understand why Chiara hadn't chosen him but had instead chosen Madeline's father. They were both Eudaizians. Kyle thought he was smart, but he couldn't seem to understand a woman's heart.

Now he was a dying creature without an identity. He was no longer Eudaizian. He wasn't Black Rock. As a creature between worlds, his essence couldn't be absorbed into any stone. His body couldn't disintegrate the way creatures' bodies did.

He lay on the scorched ground, dying the common death of an ordinary being—and his body would rot.

***

The capsule landed at the Daimon Gate. Before Ciaran could get to the children chamber, Madeline rushed to him.

He held her in his arms, and they clung to each other for a long moment. He knew what she had been through. The wait and the uncertainty were worse than physical combat.

"Look at you, Ciaran!" she said, touching his bruised face.

"I know. Tadgh said I look like shit."

"And you still helped him through the officiation process?" Madeline grinned.

He rubbed his thumb on the dimple on her left cheek. "I didn't have a choice, he's my brother. And it wasn't just me who helped him. Thanks for the signal."

She kissed him. "I'm glad you caught it," she said after the kiss. "Do you want to tell me about the explosion I saw in my vision?"

It was only a day's worth of work, but a lot had happened. He wasn't sure which explosion she referred to—the one in Black Rock or the one outside District Six.

"Hmm, it was a minor incident. I lived. That's what matters, right? How are the children?"

"Fine."

"Oh, you're back," Jennifer spoke from a corner. "Do you know how many times your wife passed out today? I discovered I am quite skilled at caring. I might get a job as a nurse."

Ciaran narrowed his eyes.

"They were psychic episodes," Madeline said.

It had happened before. Still, he didn't like the sound of it.

"Where is Moira?" Ciaran glanced around, looking for his wicked ancestor.

"Talking to your father. She's fine. You promised her something, and she seems to believe you, so she wouldn't try to snatch the children. Also, given how good I am with caring for people now, you can leave the children here. This will be the safest place in the cosmos to house your children now."

Ciaran nodded. "I agree."

"All right, off you go. I hope nothing dramatic happens before your coronation."

Ciaran smiled. It was nice to see his mother being so positive.

***

Ciaran and Madeline returned to Ciaran's Sciphil Three residence. The door slid open, welcoming them to the place they currently called home.

The home robot scurried out to greet them.

"What's the news, Robert?" Ciaran asked.

"Sciphil Seven has been successfully officiated."

"Breaking news." Madeline rolled her eyes as they entered their bedchamber.

"Negative. That was not the breaking news. The breaking news was that a district in Black Rock has been destroyed. Eudaiz has been adjusted to deal with the change in the cosmos system and reflect this destruction."

"Destruction? Wouldn't exploding Black Rock be a good thing?" Ciaran asked.

The robot said, "It would be for us. But the energy in the cosmos works on the principle of harmony. With such a large district of Black Rock vanished, we have to adjust our location and shift the natural resources."

"How about Kyle Wolf?" Madeline asked.

Robert said, "I don't have direct information. From a secondary report and information I collected, it seems Kyle was found lying in the middle of his burning house. His death has not been confirmed, but statistics suggest that with the amount of injuries he suffered, his survival chances are close to zero."

Ciaran nodded. "But not zero. I suppose that's good enough for now."

"There is an implication on you, though," said Robert.

"What now?" Ciaran snarled.

"Although Kyle was exiled, he used to be Sciphil Four. His energy remained in Tower Four. Given it is very likely he is dead, the Sciphil Four position has to be replaced or Eudaiz's power pillars will be affected and possibly collapse."

"Can we talk about this tomorrow? I need to crash right now," said Ciaran.

"Yes, of course, Ciaran. Before I leave you to your privacy, I can scan Madeline now that she isn't pregnant anymore," the robot offered.

"What? No. There's no need." Madeline waved her hands in refusal.

"This is a routine practice. Examining now will let me lock your biological age to this optimal profile."

Madeline sighed. "Okay. Skip the body index measure, though, will you? And Ciaran, can I have some privacy, please?"

Ciaran shook his head. "No. Maybe I should examine you first." He pulled her into his arms and started kissing her. His hands roamed her body, feeling unfamiliar lumps and bumps, the consequence of her childbirth. He groaned with pleasure each time he discovered something new.

"Maybe tomorrow for the scan, Robert," she said quickly to the robot. The robot didn't need another hint. It popped out the little wheels underneath its feet and raced out of the room.

END OF MINDSCAPE ONE

MINDSCAPE TWO

PART ONE

LONE CASTLE

CHAPTER 1

Jennifer peeked into the children's chamber in the capsule where her grandson and granddaughter were being safely guarded. If she believed the information she had received, this was the best technology available in the cosmos to protect children outside the mother's body.

The children's room was sealed. All she could see were monitors displaying vital signs indicating the little ones were healthy. Heartbeats. Pulses. Biological and body formation processes.

Signs of precious life.

There wasn't a window in the room, so she opened the door of the chamber to look outside.

The Daimon Gate was an independent universe. Because of its special position in multiple dimensions, this universe was the gateway between member universes. Eudaiz and Earth were the two member universes she knew well and had a close affiliation with. She had been born and raised on Earth, and the rest of her family still lived there. Her sons, Ciaran and Tadgh, now held important positions in Eudaiz.

There were thousands and thousands of member universes that the Daimon Gate managed and protected. She didn't know them all. Members connected their gateways exclusively to the Daimon Gate. That meant citizens of these universes could only travel in and out of their universes and to and from other universes with the proper passes via the Daimon Gate.

The advantage of being a member was that trespassers and enemies could be prevented from entering a member universe because there was no other way to enter and exit unless one passed the Daimon Gate's strict scanning system—a wicked and unforgiving computer called the EYE. The more members the Daimon Gate had, the safer it was for them because members would protect the only gateway connecting the multiverse.

Safety for everyone.

Jennifer's husband, Conan LeBlanc, was the Host of the Daimon Gate—the highest position and equivalent to a kingship elsewhere. And that made Jennifer the Hostess. She didn't dwell much on the position and the perks that came with it. She loved her husband, and she wanted to be with him regardless.

A wave of compressed air blew past the field in front of her, loosening dirt and unearthing young trees. A stone at the gate flipped over and rolled down the hill.

It wasn't just wind. She knew it was more than that. But she didn't have the psychic ability to see minds like her daughter-in-law, Madeline. All she had was her gut instinct, and it was telling her that multiple entities were trespassing the gate right now. She couldn't see them. She didn't know what they wanted. She just knew they were present, and they wanted something she cared about.

The children.

Before she closed the chamber door, she saw Moira walking amid the gusts toward the capsule. Moira was her five-hundred-year-old ancestor, a formidable and powerful woman who had mastered several dimensions of the multiverse, earning herself a very long life. She had been speaking with

Conan in the residence. Why was she now running back out into the wind?

Jennifer waited. Moira rushed in so fast she almost fell onto the floor. Jennifer slammed the door closed after her.

"They're coming for the children," Moira said.

"Yes. I guessed that. But what are we going to do? The children are in two gigantic boxes in a sealed room. I can't exactly scoop them up and run into the house with them."

Something smashed into the side of the chamber, which was no more than a mobile cabin without combat capability. Jennifer figured one more hit like that, and they would be rolling down the hill. "What the hell is that?" she asked.

"Haven't you been attacked before?" Moira asked.

"No. Not inside the Daimon Gate. For God's sake, if we're attacked *here*, there's nowhere in the multiverse that will be safe!" Jennifer exclaimed.

"That's a myth," Moira scoffed.

"A myth? Daimon Gate existed even before the concept of time. How can you say it's a myth?"

Another blow on the side of the chamber. It tilted. Moira darted toward the control panel and entered a series of commands. Jennifer heard humming noises from beneath them, and something snapped into place.

"We're now grounded," Moira explained, and she turned toward Jennifer. "I affixed permanent legs to the capsule. It will resist the wind and the attack outside. But I'm not sure how long it will last."

Something smashed against the chamber again. They heard the sound of claws scratching from right outside the door and walls.

"What's taking Conan so long?" Moira asked.

"What? You're not serious. He isn't leaving the residence, is he?" Jennifer asked but saw the answer on Moira's face. She rushed toward the door, but Moira snatched her away from it and swung her to the middle of the room. "If you open that door, you'll kill the children."

"If Conan makes it here, I'll have to open the door to let him in," Jennifer growled in response.

"Well, He'd better come with guards and an arsenal. At the moment, we have nothing to defend this birth chamber with," Moira snarled back.

"Why does everyone in the cosmos want the children? Yes, they're two of the best beings in existence, but so what?" Jennifer exclaimed.

"You yourself gave birth to a child of the Red Stage of the Daimon Gate. Look at how Ciaran has turned out. Look at the power he has. And now— there are twins. Of course, everyone wants them."

"Ciaran is my son. He will always be my child. I don't see any exceptional power or good it has brought him."

Moira laughed. "Don't be so sentimental . . ."

"Sentimental! You're not a mother. You'll never understand—"

An explosion cut Jennifer off. Its impact shook the chamber so severely she was afraid all the walls would cave in.

Then it went suddenly quiet.

An eerie quietness she didn't care for at all.

It was like the air and the life had been vacuumed from her surroundings. She scrambled to the door and pushed it open. The garden in front of her was a war zone. The bodies of guards littered the ground.

"Conan!" Jennifer whispered.

She charged out into the field of bodies, blood, and gore.

CHAPTER 2

Madeline gazed at the control panel and its jumble of buttons and symbols. She figured some of the buttons functioned in a way similar to the 'enter' key on her computer keyboard back on Earth. And she recognized a delete button—in her terms, the 'oops' button.

She was pretty sure the control panel operated by voice recognition. She should be able to just tell it what she wanted.

She glanced at the bed. Her husband still slept. It's not that he was a lazy sleepyhead—he was in something like a clinical state of mini-hibernation. The battles they had engaged in before arriving in Eudaiz had drained all of his natural energy, so his body now operated on a temporary artificial energy that recharged itself every night during sleep. In this universe, energy was more vital than blood.

Madeline wanted to call her mother-in-law, Jennifer, in the Daimon Gate to check on her children. But it might not be a good idea. Although Daimon Gate should be the safest place in the cosmos to hide her children, the fewer people who knew where they were, the better it was.

Calling, or holocasting—similar to a call in Eudaiz—was a sure way to publicly announce their children's whereabouts. One of their executives was a mole, and there were invisible enemies out there who wanted Ciaran dead before his coronation. It was a given that their enemies would be hunting for every single opportunity to kill him, even if it included kidnapping his children.

She sighed and gave up the idea.

Ciaran stirred and opened his eyes.

She whooshed to the bed and pressed a kiss on his face. "Good morning, warrior! How are you feeling?" She smiled.

He rubbed his thumb across her dimple and pulled her down into his arms. "Why do you have to ask me that every morning? I'm not sick, Madeline."

"Let's just accept it as my ritual morning greeting until after your coronation when you won't have to wake up every morning not knowing how much energy you've got for the day!" She grinned. "And you know what? I'm your First Councillor now, a fully operating Sciphil One. And I am a lot stronger than you."

He laughed. "A Scientist Philosopher, you are! I see you've grown to love the term!"

She loved his laughter. "Hmm, not really. Let's stick with Sciphil. I'll pretend I don't know what the word means." She played with his long, raven-black hair and noted it had grown quite a bit in the last few weeks. It nearly touched his shoulders now, making him look even more like a warrior. *Her* warrior. "Gaia dropped by earlier to check on you," Madeline said.

"Check on me? She's only a child. She shouldn't be out and about by herself in the Sciphil zone."

Madeline shrugged. "She's one smart kid, let me tell you. She went from knowing a few basic English words to speaking just like you—overnight."

Ciaran pinched Madeline's chin lightly. "What do you mean by that?"

Madeline laughed and donned her best British accent, "Well, she speaks like this. It's a cheesecake. Dark, rich Belgium chocolate with a hint of chili and strawberries." She hoped he'd laugh again. His killer grins and the way his intense eyes twinkled and focused on her when he smiled never ceased to melt her. But instead, the smile faded from Ciaran's face.

Madeline was puzzled. "I did my best with the accent. Guess I need more practice. What's wrong, Ciaran?"

"That was the dessert we had after our first dinner together in London. That was my description. You remember it."

She didn't tell him she remembered the very first moment they had collided in Hyde Park. She remembered everything—what he wore, the way he looked and spoke, and even the smell of his perspiration.

"You remember that fine detail of our first date," Ciaran repeated.

Madeline arched an eyebrow. "Yes, I have a good memory. Why is that a big deal?"

Ciaran shook his head and sat up. "Sometimes it's better to just forget," he mumbled and headed toward the bathroom.

An image flashed in her mind. Her psychic ability switched on, and she saw Ciaran's mind. It was rare for her to see it out of the blue. And especially when nothing significant was happening. Or *was* there something significant happening?

"We've come up with the name Caedmon for our son. But we don't have a girl's name yet, Ciaran. How about Lyla?"

That was the word she had just seen in his mind. He turned around slowly. The look on his face made her want to recoil. But she didn't. She manufactured a smile. "What do you think?"

"Anything but Lyla."

His voice was so low, it came out more like a hiss.

"But I like that name. If you don't, can you tell me why?"

He shook his head and strode out of the room.

"Don't walk away from me, Ciaran." She raised her voice. "There can't be secrets between us. Not back on Earth. And especially not here . . . not . . ." It might have been her tone, what she said, or the fact the she started to breathe heavily as if she was in shock that stopped Ciaran in his tracks.

The precognition hit her liked a tidal wave. In front of her was a flash of images.

Blood.

Zombies.

Snakes.

Space creatures.

And Conan—Ciaran's father—covered in blood. In her vision, she pushed the monsters away to save Conan. But there were so many of them. Without a weapon, she couldn't do much.

She pushed and shoved, but it had no effect on the monsters.

She cried.

And then she was floating. Ciaran was shaking her. She opened her eyes and found herself in his arms, and she saw the terror on his face. The thin material of his sleeping shirt had been torn. She saw trails of blood on his chest where she had scratched him.

He wiped the tears from her face. "I'm sorry. Don't cry. Let me take you to bed."

He carried her to bed and wrapped her up in a blanket. Her teeth chattered uncontrollably, and she couldn't even speak. He climbed onto the bed and held her tightly. She could feel his muscles quivering as much as her own. She could feel the vibration of his anxiety. She knew he suffered from her vision as much as she did even though he didn't have any psychic abilities and hadn't seen what she'd seen.

After a while, her temperature evened out. Ciaran looked at her and asked, "I guess this was one of your psychic episodes?"

She nodded.

"If it's this bad, then we have to do something about it," he said.

"I saw—"

He locked her lips with a deep kiss to cut her off. When he finished, he said, "Whatever terrible thing you saw, we'll fix it. Okay? I want you to know that."

She nodded again. Before she could say anything further, a robotic announcement broadcast from the speaker.

"You have a holocast from Jennifer LeBlanc."

"Accept," Ciaran said.

"Affirmative," the robot said.

Then Jennifer's voice came across, "Ciaran, your father's in trouble. Come at once."

CHAPTER 3

Everyone called him Master. He liked it. Creatures in space, humans on Earth, and paranormal creatures feared him, at least those he was in contact with. He had never told them his name, so he was happy their fear translated into the name Master.

He was the master of many things. But sorcery was his forte.

It had been hundreds of years that he had walked the cosmos, living in multiple dimensions and multiple universes. He had no place he could call home, but there was one place he wanted—Eudaiz.

Among the many things he couldn't have, Eudaiz had always been his most desirable goal and the most painful failure he had ever experienced in his very long and unnatural life.

Unlike the many pathetic creatures he hired, he would never give up. One day, he *would* take his rightful place in Eudaiz, and he was willing to do whatever it took to get there. He had sacrificed enough. There had always been one hurdle between him and Eudaiz—the LeBlancs. But he'd learned his lesson. This time, he would be successful.

He would be where he deserved to be.

He wiped the gore of Kyle's body, a remnant of the explosion, from his hands. "You're useless," he muttered. The tasks he had given Kyle were simple—capture the children and replace Sciphil Seven.

Kyle had failed both jobs.

Now he would have to get his hands dirty and handle some trivial matters.

He shook his head.

There had been too many errors, and the coronation date had crept up faster than he wanted.

There were too many things to do and not enough reliable creatures in the multiverse to hire.

He turned on his communication channel, blocked the visual, and called his spy in Eudaiz. "Give me some good news," he said.

***

As soon as the capsule landed and he verified his palm print on the control panel, Ciaran strode straight to the gate of his parents' residence in the Daimon Gate. Madeline was right beside him. She always was. And he would need all of her support very soon.

The grand reception room reeked of the stench of blood. The bodies of guards were everywhere. Blood smears painted the room. On the shiny white floor. On the polished marble benches. On the white walls decorated with classical paintings. And on the glass of the windows.

Jennifer stormed in from the hallway. Ciaran rushed over to hold his mother. He knew she would never allow any sign of weakness to show. But at the moment, fear had taken over his mother. She was incoherent. So he did what a son should do. He comforted her.

Ciaran signaled Madeline. She came to stand next to Jennifer. Ciaran turned on the control panel to check the computer system. The computer didn't detect the carnage. It thought everything was operating normally, and that Conan was most likely relaxing in the room, drinking his tea.

"Do you sense any Black Rock creatures here, Madeline?" Ciaran asked.

"No," she answered.

"The computer detects nothing," he muttered.

"It was a tremendous explosion. The gusts from it almost blew your children's chamber away. How can the computer see *nothing?*" Jennifer exclaimed.

"The attackers were invisible to the system. The EYE is the most sophisticated computer system in the cosmos. If it can't detect the creatures, your gate security has no hope."

Jennifer flopped down heavily in a chair. "It was my fault," she cried. "I was always thinking of Eudaiz. If things went wrong, it had something to do with Eudaiz. If someone attacked us, it was because of Eudaiz. There are nine thousand gates within the Daimon Gate, and each one is connected to thousands of universes. But I've never thought much about them. I left the residence defenseless and locked myself in the children's birth chamber because I thought that was what they had come for."

Ciaran crouched next to his mother and held her hands. "You're not thinking straight, Mother. Eudaiz is the most prosperous universe. Of course it's the most likely target for attack. Go easy on yourself."

"If they targeted Eudaiz, they must be the Black Rock, right? Can you go there and bring your father back? You've been there before to rescue Tadgh."

"Madeline didn't sense any Black Rock creatures in here."

"But if it wasn't them, then who else?" Then Jennifer looked behind Ciaran. "Where's your brother? Why isn't Tadgh with you?"

"Mother, Tadgh has just taken his Sciphil Seven position. He's still in training. I didn't tell him anything yet."

"Your father is missing, and you didn't think to tell your brother? I know Conan isn't your real father, but he brought you up, and he's the only father you know."

He knew his mother wasn't thinking straight. But he didn't expect what she was saying would hurt him so much. "Mother, you're being unreasonable."

Madeline pushed her way in and held his mother's shoulders so she looked straight into Madeline's eyes. She said, "You know I have psychic ability. I told you it wasn't Black Rock creatures. If you insist that Ciaran go to Black Rock, it will be a waste of time and effort."

Ciaran turned away from his mother. He looked out to the garden where he had parked the birth chamber of their children, and his blood ran cold. His mother had left Moira, his wicked ancestor with a vested interest in the children, alone in the birth chamber.

Saying nothing, Ciaran darted out of the house toward the chamber.

***

Moira turned around and smiled at Ciaran when he stormed into the room. In the confined space, he could feel the vibration of her energy. Her formidability and authority would have overwhelmed any creature in the cosmos.

"You were afraid I'd take your children, Ciaran?"

"I trust no one when it comes them."

"Well, you don't have much of a choice, do you? You can't take soldiers into the Daimon Gate. Now that your father's been taken, will you go and rescue him, or stay here and guard your children . . . against me? We have an agreement, Ciaran. If you hold up your end, I will mine. Your mother isn't thinking straight right now. But you are the king-to-be of Eudaiz. You cannot let your judgment be clouded by such trivial matters."

"My father is missing. That's not trivial. Not to me personally, and not to the Daimon Gate and the safety of the cosmos. If he is held for ransom, it will be catastrophic."

"Not really," Moira said matter-of-factly. "If Conan is held against the interest of the cosmos, he will kill himself. That's just a necessary responsibility of a man in his position."

Ciaran punched the wall so hard it shook loose a wooden panel.

Moira continued, "Human emotion is your weakness, Ciaran. You have to get it under control, or you'll be in serious trouble."

"I know what I'm capable of. I don't need your advice," Ciaran snarled as Madeline and Jennifer stormed in.

"How is quarreling going to help the situation?" Jennifer raised her voice.

"He's upset because you weren't thinking straight. Don't blame that on me, Jennifer," Moira said.

Jennifer sighed. "I'm sorry. I didn't mean what I said about . . . Conan."

Ciaran turned around and looked at his mother. "He's the father I've known my whole life. And he will always be my father. But he didn't give me my life—"

"I know, and I said I'm sorry, Ciaran," Jennifer cut in.

Ciaran nodded. Moira was right. He was too emotional about this. He was glad his mother had cut in. Otherwise, he could easily have ranted on and on about the fact that he'd had to kill Bran, his real father, for Conan. He didn't regret it. He had done what he had to do. But he would never forgive himself for doing it.

Madeline walked toward the two boxes that contained her twins. She traced her hands across the glass panel. Ciaran approached from behind. He removed her hands and held them in his. "Our children will be fine, Madeline."

"I'll look after them when you leave to rescue Conan," Moira said. "How many guards do you have left, Jennifer?"

Jennifer shook her head. "We don't have any residential guards left alive. But we have hundreds of thousands of guards at the gate at our disposal. All I have to do is to call the committee."

"Don't," Ciaran said. "If you call the Daimon Gate committee and tell them their leader is missing, you'll spread confusion and fear. That's a recipe for chaos and will lead to disastrous consequences. It might be exactly what Father's kidnapper wants."

"Welcome back, Ciaran," Moira smiled. "Precisely. The Daimon Gate is the only secure gateway to the multiverse for thousands of universes. If an outside universe wants to invade those member universes of the Daimon Gate, they will need the Daimon Gate to be vulnerable. Chaos is the best strategy to weaken it. And capturing Conan is a good way to create chaos—*if* we give in to what they want."

"I've been to the Black Rock. I've seen their creatures. They don't have the capacity to pull this off," Ciaran said.

Moira shook her head. "It's not the Black Rock. It's far worse."

For a limited time, D.N. Leo gives away
4 books in the Multiverse Collection

CLAIM YOUR FREE E-BOOKS
http://narrativeland.com

THANK YOU FOR READING!
D.N. LEO

D.N. LEO 'S NOVELS
SERIES READING ORDER

http://www.narrativeland.com/dnleo-series-reading-order

—

A SHADE OF MIND
(narrativeland.com/shade)
Main Characters: Ciaran, Madeline, Tadgh, and Jo
(Recommended reading in order)
1-4 Random Psychic
2-4 Forever Mortal
3-4 Elusive Beings
4-4 Imperfect Divine

—

SPECTRUM
(narrativeland.com/spectrum)
Main characters: Lorcan, Orla, Roy and Mori
(Recommended reading in order)
1-4 White Curse
2-4 Blue Fox
3-4 Indigo Stone
4-4 Red Moon

—

MINDSCAPE
(narrativeland.com/mind)
Main characters:
Ciaran, Madeline, Tadgh, Jo, Kyle, Hoyt, Ayana, Pete,
Sizx, Lorcan, Orla
(Recommended reading in order within series, can be
read in ANY order in related to other series)

Queen's Gambit
Knight & Pawn
Lone Castle
Doubled Bishops
Dead Squares
King's Endgame

—

SILVER BLOOD
Main characters:
(narrativeland.com/silver)
Ciaran, Madeline, Tadgh, Jo, Caedmon, Sedna, Roy,
Mori, Zach, Mya, Lorcan and Orla
This series can be read in ANY order within the series
and in related to other series.

Virgo
Libra
Scorpio
Taurus
Pisces
Gemini

323

Thank you for reading.

If you enjoyed reading **Mindscape One**, I would appreciate it if you would help others enjoy this book, too.

Recommend it. Please help other readers find this book by recommending it to friends, readers' groups and discussion boards.

Review it. Please tell other readers why you liked this book by reviewing it wherever you purchase the book from. If you do write a review, please send me an email at info@dnleo.com so I can thank you with a personal email.

COPYRIGHT

MINDSCAPE ONE

By D.N. Leo